'I don't do simple, straightforward paintings.'

Maxim's dark eyes locked onto her face again. 'And you are going to strip bare for me, Cleo. Oh, I [illegible] lly,' he added, as he saw the su[illegible]. 'I mean that, [illegible] eventually goin[illegible] soul. And *that'*[illegible] r portrait.'

He then [illegible] oom.

Dear Reader

Easter is upon us, and with it our thoughts turn to the meaning of Easter. For many, it's a time when Nature gives birth to all things, so what better way to begin a new season of love and romance than by reading some of the new authors whom we have recently introduced to our lists? Watch out for Helen Brooks, Jenny Cartwright, Liz Fielding, Sharon Kendrick and Catherine O'Connor—all of whom have books coming out this spring!

The Editor

Joanna Mansell hasn't always wanted to write. It was an idea that popped into her head when she was 'thirty-something', and then wouldn't go away again. It's turned out to be rather addictive, though, and now she has started, she says, she can't stop! When she's not working, she loves reading, gardening, watching films, day-dreaming, and sneaking away from the typewriter on hot, sunny days to go for walks along the sea front.

Recent titles by the same author:

SECRETS OF THE NIGHT

PORTRAIT OF CLEO

BY

JOANNA MANSELL

MILLS & BOON LIMITED
ETON HOUSE 18-24 PARADISE ROAD
RICHMOND SURREY TW9 1SR

First published in Great Britain 1993
by Mills & Boon Limited

This edition 1993

ISBN 0 263 77976 9

Set in Times Roman 10 on 12 pt.
01-9304-53600 C

Made and printed in Great Britain

CHAPTER ONE

CLEO ran her fingers through the silky, pale blonde strands of her hair and then looked at her father with exasperation. 'How could you have made all these arrangements without even consulting me?'

'You were out of the country on a modelling assignment,' her father reminded her. 'I did try to telephone you, but I couldn't get through.'

She shot a suspicious glance at him. 'Are you sure you tried very hard? The phones in Bermuda usually work without too many problems.'

'There must have been some local trouble with the lines,' her father replied smoothly. 'Anyway, I thought you wouldn't mind. I checked with your agent, and he said that you didn't have any more work lined up until the end of the month.'

'That's because I was planning to take a break! I've been working solidly right through the summer. I need a few days off. I *don't* need my portrait painted.'

'You can relax in between sittings,' her father said at once. 'And the Lake District is ideal for a short break. All those mountains, the fresh air, the scenery—I'm sure you'll like it.'

'It rains a great deal in the Lake District,' Cleo said pointedly.

'You've been complaining all summer that they keep sending you on photographic assignments to places that are too hot and too sunny.'

'That doesn't mean that I want to go somewhere really wet, *and* have to sit around while someone paints my portrait.'

'I know. But I still want you to do it.'

'Why?' asked Cleo, with a fresh burst of exasperation. 'You've got dozens of photos of me, and I can easily get you more, as many as you want.'

'Even the best photograph in the world can't capture someone in the same way that a good portrait painting can.' Her father's face and voice altered. 'It's your twenty-third birthday at the end of the month, Cleo. I want this painting to hang alongside the one I already have of your mother.'

Cleo swallowed hard, and realised rather belatedly that she had been very stupid—and unfeeling. If she hadn't still been feeling rather jet-lagged after the long flight from Bermuda, she would have realised a lot sooner why her father had suddenly decided that he wanted a portrait of her.

Her twenty-third birthday—the same age her mother had been when she had married Cleo's father. Her father had had the portrait of his new wife specially commissioned, to celebrate their wedding. Nine months later, Cleo had been born, a honeymoon baby. And, just five years later, her mother had died a few days after giving birth to a stillborn child. There had been complications, and she hadn't had enough strength left to pull through. Since then, there had been just Cleo and her father, closer than most fathers and daughters because they had only had each other. Her father had never remarried, and Cleo had had boyfriends but had never been involved in any really serious relationship; had never found anyone who could quite measure up to the powerful, strong-willed man who had raised her.

'I've made a lot of enquiries over the past couple of weeks,' her father was now telling her, 'and when it comes to portrait painting there's one man who stands head and shoulders above the rest. Maxim Brenner. He's even done a couple of royal portraits. I've seen examples of his work and they're good, *very* good. The only problem I had was in persuading him to accept this commission. His work's very much in demand, he's booked up for months ahead. I finally persuaded him to fit you in, though.'

Cleo's well shaped eyebrows quirked upwards. She knew how persuasive her father could be when he set his mind to it!

'He couldn't spare the time to come down here to London, though,' her father went on. 'That's why you've got to go up to his house, in the Lake District. He's agreed to let you stay there for a few days, until the portrait's finished. He's got a self-contained annexe where clients stay when they're sitting for portraits.'

'A few days?' echoed Cleo in dismay. 'Will it really take that long?'

'Good portraits can't be dashed off in an afternoon. And, as I said, he's an extremely busy man. He's going to work on your picture whenever he's got a couple of free hours, so he can't say exactly how long it's going to take.'

'Can't I just go up there for an odd half-day now and then, for sittings?'

'He doesn't know in advance when he's going to be free. That's why he wants you there at the house, so you're available for sittings whenever he can fit you in. Anyway, it wouldn't be practical to commute between London and Cumbria; it's a six-hundred-mile round trip.'

'Isn't there someone in London who could do a portrait that's just as good?' she said hopefully.

'I want the best,' her father said firmly. 'And Maxim Brenner *is* the best.' Then he gave a faint frown. 'I suppose I ought to warn you that he's got a reputation for being rather difficult. Among other things, he insists on keeping total control over the portraits he produces.'

'Oh, great,' said Cleo wryly.

'I don't think you'll have any problem dealing with him. You probably won't even see very much of him in between sittings. But please remember, this portrait means a lot to me.' His tone altered as he went on, 'I've never told you this before, but when you were born your mother and I promised each other that we would have your portrait painted when you reached your twenty-third birthday. You know that's how old your mother was when she married me, and had you, her first child. We planned to hang your portrait alongside hers, mother and daughter at the same age. Keeping that promise means a lot to me, Cleo. But I can't do it without your co-operation.'

'Why didn't you tell me all this before?' she asked in a subdued voice.

'Because I know that you find it painful to talk about your mother. So do I,' he admitted frankly. 'Will you do this for me? Go to Cumbria and stay at Maxim Brenner's house until he's finished the portrait?'

'Of course I will,' she said at once. 'When do I have to go?'

'Tomorrow. He wants you there as soon as possible, because he's got a couple of free afternoons this week.'

Cleo couldn't help giving a faint groan. She had been hoping for a couple of days at home first.

'But I haven't even unpacked the things I brought back from Bermuda!'

'Take them with you,' advised her father. 'It'll save repacking.'

'I don't think I'll be needing bikinis, thin cotton tops and shorts. I told you, it *rains* in the Lake District. I'd better take a mac, lots of jumpers and waterproof boots,' she said, wrinkling her nose.

'You'll enjoy it once you're there. And I don't think it rains every single minute of the day and night!' Her father hesitated, then added in a rather different tone of voice, 'I'm very grateful that you've agreed to do this, Cleo.'

She gave him a rueful smile. 'You know that I always do what you want me to do.' And that was the truth. Ever since she could remember, she had always wanted to please her father. 'And I promise I'll stay until the portrait's finished, no matter how difficult Maxim Brenner turns out to be,' she added.

He looked rather relieved, as if he hadn't expected her to give in so easily. They had their evening meal together, and then Cleo went upstairs to pack. Tomorrow she would be heading north to the Lake District—and Maxim Brenner.

Cleo's small red sports car—a twenty-first birthday present from her father—sped noisily along the motorway. And it *was* raining! The further north she went, the harder it pelted against the windscreen.

Cleo gave a resigned sigh. It's only for a few days, she reminded herself. Then she could go home again, and spend what was left of her holiday just relaxing and pampering herself. At the end of the month it would be her twenty-third birthday. She would stay at home until then, to celebrate her birthday with her father, and then it would be back to work again. Her agent already had a couple of photographic assignments lined up, one in Paris and one in London. And there was a good chance that she would be spearheading the campaign for a new perfume that was being launched in the new year. Her face fitted the image that they wanted, and before leaving for Bermuda she had done a screen-test for a commercial, which had apparently worked out well.

She knew that she ought to be very pleased with her life at the moment. At twenty-three, her unmarked skin and clear green eyes were still good enough to stand up to even the closest scrutiny by the cameras. She earned very good money, she often travelled to exotic locations on different modelling assignments, and the future looked very bright, particularly if they did finally decide that hers was the face they wanted to launch the new perfume.

So, why didn't she feel more cheerful? Why had there been that faint cloud of depression hanging over her lately?

Cleo bit her lip because she thought that she already knew the answer to those questions. Her life didn't seem to be *going* anywhere. She had a successful career, money, looks, even fame of a sort, but somehow it wasn't enough. That made her feel guilty, because she was very aware that she had the kind of lifestyle a lot of people would kill for. So why wasn't it enough for her? What was missing?

She gave an impatient shake of her head. Nothing was missing, she told herself firmly. She was just feeling rather down at the moment, for some reason. Perhaps she had been working too hard. She had to forget about it, think about something else.

She let her mind drift to the portrait of her mother that hung in the drawing-room. Cleo had inherited her blonde hair from her mother, although her green eyes had come from her father. From that portrait, she knew that her mother had had brown eyes, kind, gentle eyes. Cleo desperately wished that she could clearly remember for herself what her mother had looked like. She had been five years old when her mother had died, she had memories of her voice, her softness, even her smell, but Cleo just couldn't picture her face. She had tried and tried, but the memory seemed to have been completely wiped out. She supposed that it was the shock of losing her mother so suddenly. She remembered being told that there was a new baby coming, she even remembered looking forward excitedly to her mother and the baby coming home from the hospital. Then there had been that awful afternoon when her father had gently told her that there wouldn't be any baby. And, worse than that, so much worse, her mother would never be coming home again.

Cleo gave a small shudder. Even after all this time, the faint echoes of shock and disbelief could still hit her. And it had also left her with a phobic fear of hospitals and of childbirth. She looked after her own health almost obsessively because she lived in dread of becoming ill and having to be admitted to hospital. And she had decided long ago that she was *never* going to have children. She knew very well that the risks involved were small, but they were still there. If they weren't, her mother would still be alive! And, since she didn't intend to have children, there didn't seem any point in getting married. Anyway, she didn't need to marry, she told herself rather defiantly. She was financially independent, she had a good career, and she and her father shared a house—

and their lives—without any problems. There was no reason why she should change her lifestyle in any way.

The car roared on, the rain pelted down more heavily, and Cleo forced herself to concentrate on the road. She had to turn off the motorway soon, and head north-westwards into the Lake District. Her father had given her detailed instructions on how to reach Maxim Brenner's house, but in this filthy weather it would be very easy to get lost.

After she had left the motorway, low hills began to loom out of the mist and wet sheep huddled miserably against hedges, trying to shelter from the worst of the rain. Although it was only mid afternoon, the light was so bad that it seemed more like early evening. Cleo felt her depression returning in full force, and wished she had somehow found the courage to tell her father that she really didn't want to do this. For some reason, it made her feel funny inside to think of her portrait hanging alongside the painting of her mother. Too late now, though. She had promised, and she had never broken a promise to her father.

She would feel better if the weather weren't so gloomy, she told herself. The endless rain, the grey mist—she found herself suddenly longing for the bright, cheerful sunshine of Bermuda.

The road skirted round Windermere and its rain-soaked tourists, and then wound past the northern end of the lake to Ambleside, and its congested one-way system. Cleo could feel herself growing tired and frustrated as she pushed on along roads that were becoming increasingly narrow and winding. A couple of times she stopped to consult the map her father had given her, and once missed a half-hidden turn off, so she had to turn the car round—not at all easy on a narrow road with a ditch running along one side!—and retrace the route.

Maxim Brenner must live in one of the most isolated parts of this sodden corner of England! she decided with an irritable frown. Why couldn't he live somewhere more civilised?

One last turn off led her down a tree-lined lane, and at the end of it she could finally see the dark silhouette of a house. It was much bigger than she had expected, and looked rather forbidding, looming out of the sheets of rain.

Cleo brought the car to a halt on the gravel drive and then tooted the horn, to let Maxim Brenner know that she had arrived. She wanted him to open the front door so that she could dash inside without getting too wet.

The door stayed shut, though. There were no signs of life inside the house, not even the faint twitching of a curtain to show that someone had noticed her arrival.

'Oh, great,' she muttered to herself. That meant she was going to get soaked while she knocked on the front door.

With an exaggerated sigh, Cleo pulled her thin cotton jacket more tightly around her. She had brought a mac, but it was packed away in her suitcase, in the boot. By the time she had fished it out she would be drenched to the skin.

She opened the car door and made a dash for the front entrance. Then she thumped on the knocker very hard, at the same time shaking raindrops from her hair and clothes.

No one came to open the door, and Cleo became steadily more exasperated. What was going on here? Maxim Brenner knew she was coming, her father had phoned to tell him that she would be arriving mid-afternoon. He couldn't possibly have gone out—could he?

She hammered on the door again, and then gave it a small kick of frustration when it remained closed. 'This is *not* a good start,' she muttered under her breath.

She stepped back and looked up at the house, trying to see if any windows were open. The exterior of the house had a closed, almost empty look, though. It was hard to believe that anyone actually lived here.

Cleo was tempted to give up straight away and drive directly back to London. After all, she couldn't be expected to stay here if there wasn't anyone at home, could she? She had even taken a couple of steps back to the car when she remembered her promise to her father. What was he going to say when he found out that she hadn't even tried to get inside the house? That she had knocked on the door a couple of times and then walked away?

A small sigh escaped her. She supposed she ought to try a little harder than this to get someone to realise she was here.

Knocking on the front door was obviously useless. Either Maxim Brenner was out, or he was working in another part of the house and couldn't hear her.

Cleo wrinkled her nose. What to try next? Maybe there was a back entrance to the house, and she could get in that way, she finally decided.

By the time she had made her way round to the rear of the house, though, she was soaked through and her pale hair was plastered to her scalp. The rain was falling down in great sheets.

Round the back, there was a small courtyard surrounded on three sides by the dark, looming bulk of the house. This really was a very cheerless place, she told herself as she squelched towards the door that opened on to the courtyard. Perhaps Maxim Brenner was one of those dark, brooding artists, moody and temperamental, so wrapped up in his work that he paid little attention to his surroundings. After all, her father had warned her that he was difficult.

It was also difficult to get into his house! Cleo splashed through the puddles that filled the courtyard, muttering balefully under her breath as water dripped down her neck, poured into her shoes and soaked through her clothes. When she finally reached the door that led into the house, she didn't even bother to knock. She tried the handle, and when she found that it turned she opened the door and marched straight inside.

She found herself in a large kitchen. A door let out the far side, and she went through it, to find herself in a long hallway, with several more doors leading off it.

'Where do I go now?' she said out loud, with growing impatience.

Then a door to her left abruptly opened and a tall, dark figure appeared directly in front of her.

'You're late,' growled a male voice. 'Take your clothes off and lie down on the couch. I'll be with you in a couple of minutes.'

He disappeared through one of the other doors while Cleo was still gaping at him. 'Take my clothes off?' she whispered to herself in disbelief. Then she felt a fast growing sense of outrage. 'Who—or *what*—does he think I am?'

Then the man reappeared, as swiftly as before. Cleo tried to say something, but he gripped hold of her arm and propelled her into the nearby room.

'You're still not undressed,' he said with a fierce frown. 'Get your things off as quickly as you can. I don't have much time.'

Cleo finally found her voice. 'I'm not taking my clothes off for you, or for anyone!' she said furiously.

She found herself pinned down by dark eyes that blazed with pure exasperation.

'Then why did you come here? I made it very clear what I required of you.'

Her own tone became absolutely icy as she drew herself up to her full height and stared back at him with freezing dislike.

'I don't know who you think I am, but you've made a very big mistake.'

'You're not willing to take your clothes off?'

'There isn't anything in this world that would make me undress in front of you!'

The man's rather grim mouth relaxed just a fraction. 'I was only offering money and I intended to pay the standard rate,' he said drily.

Sheer outrage spread over Cleo's face again. 'I've no idea what the "standard rate" is, but I feel very sorry for any poor girl who has to do this kind of thing for money!'

'There's clearly been some mix-up,' he said, after a short pause. 'You're obviously not the girl I thought you were. But, just out of interest, exactly what did you think I wanted this girl to do?'

To Cleo's intense annoyance she could feel a red flush creeping over her skin. 'That seems fairly obvious,' she retorted. 'What does any man have in mind after he's got a girl to undress and lie down on the couch?'

'I can't speak for other men, but I can certainly tell you what *I* had in mind. I wanted her to lie very still, holding a particular pose, while I painted her.'

Cleo swallowed very hard. 'P-painted her?' she said at last, in a small voice.

'I phoned up the local art college earlier, and they arranged for one of their life models to come over for a couple of hours this afternoon to pose for me.'

The man had moved closer while he was speaking, and she swallowed hard again. She was only a couple of inches short of six foot, but he still seemed to tower over her. That was a new experience for Cleo. She was used to facing men on more equal terms.

'You're—you're Maxim Brenner?' she said a little shakily.

'And you're the rich bitch who wants her portrait painted,' he said in a not particularly pleasant tone. 'I forgot you were coming.'

'How could you forget?' she said with fresh indignation. 'My father made the arrangements only a couple of days ago. And I think you should treat me a little better than this,' she added, in a rather haughty tone. 'He's paying you very handsomely for this portrait.'

Maxim's dark eyes became almost black. 'And you think that gives you certain rights and privileges?' he said softly.

His tone of voice made every one of her nerve ends silently quiver. Cleo stood her ground, though. This was one argument she was sure she could win. Her father had taught her the enormous advantages that come with enormous wealth.

'Money always gives you privileges,' she said confidently.

His gaze locked on to her own. 'Not in this house.'

'It got me in here, didn't it?' she challenged him, wondering how she was finding the nerve to stand up to this intimidating man. 'What did my father do? Offer you twice the going rate for a portrait? He always says everyone has his price.'

Warning lines appeared around Maxim Brenner's mouth. 'You think that I'm for sale?'

'Why not?' Cleo said rashly. 'After all, you have agreed to paint my portrait, haven't you? He must have found some way of persuading you.'

This time, Maxim didn't reply. Got him! Cleo thought. He couldn't answer her without admitting that he had taken some kind of bribe.

She had no idea why it was so important to get the better of this man. Or why these sparks of sheer antagonism had been flying between them ever since they had set eyes on each other. She didn't usually react like this to someone she had just met. In fact, she couldn't remember anything quite like this happening before.

It was just beginning to occur to her that it wasn't very sensible to behave like this, since she was going to have to stay in Maxim Brenner's house for the next few days, when he slid his fingers around her upper arm, and began to march her towards the door.

'What are you doing?' she said in sudden alarm.

His dark eyes glittered. 'What do you think I'm doing?'

'I've no idea,' Cleo said rather breathlessly, as he relentlessly forced her along the hall. 'But you'd better take your hands off me *right now*. If my father ever hears that you've treated me like this——'

'Your father is three hundred miles away, in London,' he pointed out. 'And perhaps I'm only doing something that he should have done long ago.'

'He would never manhandle me!' she said furiously.

'I'm not manhandling you, I'm simply holding your arm. But if I were your father—and thank God I'm not!—I'd have made very sure that I taught you some basic manners, even if it meant that I occasionally had to paddle your backside until you were too sore to sit down.'

They reached the kitchen and Maxim propelled her swiftly through it, towards the back door.

'You're not——?' she began suspiciously.

'Throwing you out?' A taut smile touched his mouth. 'But that's exactly what I'm doing.'

'It's pouring rain out there!'

'That isn't my problem.'

'You can't do this,' Cleo said in outraged voice.

'Of course I can. This is my house, I can do whatever I damned well please. You can come back in when you're ready to apologise for your rudeness and agree to keep a civil tongue in your head.'

'I'm never going to do that!'

'Then you can stay out there indefinitely,' Maxim Brenner said coolly. And, as he finished speaking, he pushed her out into the courtyard and closed the door behind her.

The rain fell down on Cleo's unprotected head and steadily began to soak through her still damp clothes. She gave a furious frown and turned away from the door. All right, she had given it a try and it hadn't worked out. That surely meant she was no longer bound by that promise she had given to her father? After all, Maxim Brenner hadn't just turned out to be difficult, he was impossible! She conveniently ignored the fact that the whole thing hadn't been exactly one-sided. She had been tired from the journey, she argued with herself. He should have been ready to make allowances because of that. And, of course, she had been completely thrown off balance when he had ordered her to take her clothes off. He hadn't even said that he was *sorry* for that little incident and the mistake he had made!

Cleo lifted her head defiantly. No, she certainly hadn't been at fault. And she definitely wasn't going to be the one who was going to apologise!

She would drive straight back to London and try to explain to her father why she hadn't been able to stay. He would just have to find another portrait painter if he really wanted this painting of her.

She marched round to the car, reaching into the pocket of her sodden cotton jacket for the keys. They weren't there! Cleo stood very still because she suddenly remembered where she had left them. When she had first gone into the house, she had been holding them in her hand. And she had put them down on the table in the kitchen.

They were still there. She couldn't drive back to London. She couldn't even sit in the car, out of the rain, because she had locked it when she had got out.

Frustration swept over her and she stamped her foot. Unfortunately, she was standing in a puddle, and more water splashed up her legs and dribbled into her shoes. It really was the last straw. For a few moments, she could actually feel tears prickling at the back of her eyes.

Cleo knew that she might not have over-reacted quite so much if she hadn't been so totally *wet*. Even her undies were starting to feel damp as the rain soaked steadily through her clothes.

For a few moments, she actually contemplated walking out of here. The only trouble was, Maxim Brenner seemed to live miles from the nearest signs of civilisation. She could tramp around for hours in this pouring rain before she reached a village or small town. And on top of that, she was wearing light fashion shoes that definitely weren't designed for long-distance walking.

Cleo gritted her teeth as she considered the alternative—knocking on that door and apologising to Maxim Brenner.

'I can't do it,' she muttered to herself. 'I simply cannot *do* it.'

But after another ten minutes of pacing furiously around in the drenching rain, with water dribbling down inside her clothes and her saturated shoes practically disintegrating, she began to think that she might just be able to do it, after all. And five minutes later, she was standing in front of the door, forcing herself to knock on it.

Maxim opened it almost at once. 'Do you have something to say to me?' he asked calmly.

Cleo looked straight at him and realised, with a small sense of shock, that he was an astonishingly good-looking man. During that first encounter, she had really only taken in the darkness of his eyes, the blackness of his hair, and his rather intimidating height. Now, though, she noticed his elegant bone-structure, the fine line of his nose and the severe yet sensual, curve of his mouth.

She swallowed rather harder than was strictly necessary.

'I—er——' She coughed, and tried again. 'I want to apologise for my rudeness,' she mumbled.

To her relief, he opened the door wider and let her come inside. As soon as she was out of the rain, she began to feel better. She also began to feel indignant all over again.

'You had no right shutting me out like that,' she said, turning round to face him.

'I've the right to choose who I let into my house,' Maxim said coolly.

'But look at me. I'm soaked right through to the skin!'

'If you'd worn sensible clothes, you'd have stayed fairly dry,' he said without the slightest trace of sympathy.

'I didn't know I was going to have to stand outside for an hour in the pouring rain!'

'It was less than fifteen minutes, and you wouldn't have had to stand out there at all if you'd been prepared to apologise straight away.'

'I didn't think that I needed to apologise at all,' Cleo retorted at once. 'As soon as I came in, you told me to take my clothes off and lie down on the couch! How was I *supposed* to react to that?'

His dark eyes showed a brief glimmer of amusement. 'I've no idea. How do you usually react to that kind of invitation?'

'I turn it down!' she said furiously. Then she realised that he was having fun, at her expense. That made her even more angry.

'Look, this obviously isn't going to work,' she went on, glaring at him. She grabbed hold of her car keys, which were still lying on the kitchen table. 'I'm going back to London. As far as I'm concerned, the portrait has been cancelled. I suppose that my father paid you some kind of advance, but you'll just have to return it to him.'

'That's impossible,' Maxim told her. 'I've already used the money. And, if you're interested, your father didn't give me an advance. He's already paid in full for your portrait—and I'm afraid that it's cost him a great deal of money.'

Cleo blinked. 'And you've already spent every penny of it?' she said, in disbelief.

'Why not? What's the point of leaving money lying around in the bank doing nothing?'

'You'll have to find some way of reimbursing him,' she said indignantly.

'I've no intention of doing that,' Maxim told her, his dark eyes fixing on her levelly. 'Your father understood that, if the portrait didn't work out for any reason, there was no question of his money being returned.'

'My father would never enter into an agreement like that!'

'He already has. I set my terms out very clearly, and he was more than willing to go along with them.'

Cleo bit her lip. Did her father really want this portrait so much that he was willing to accept virtually any terms in order to get it?

Her green eyes became troubled. Her father was a very wealthy man, and no matter how large a sum he had paid to Maxim Brenner, he could easily afford to lose it. She hated to see him cheated in any way, though. And if he lost the money *and* ended up without the portrait he wanted so much, then it would be all her fault. She would be the one who had messed this up, and all because she couldn't get along with Maxim Brenner.

She didn't even understand why she couldn't get along with him, why they were having all these problems when they had only just met. All right, so he was a difficult man—her father had warned her that he would be. But she had encountered difficult men before—the modelling world was well known for having more than its fair share of temperamental people!—and she had always managed to charm them, and smooth over any small difficulties.

Cleo shot a quick glance at Maxim and then gave a small frown. Perhaps it was because he didn't *look* the way she had expected an artist to look. She had had a rather stereotyped image in her mind, of someone with shaggy hair, old paint-stained clothes and a bohemian outlook on life. Maxim's black hair was beautifully cut, his clothes were casual but still managed to look extremely expensive, and he obviously applied very strict rules when it came to such things as behaviour and good manners.

As well as that, he didn't seem in the least impressed by the way *she* looked. Cleo wasn't used to that. With her big green eyes, pale blonde hair and tall, willowy body, she was accustomed to men being very impressed indeed! She knew very well that her face and figure gave her a lot of unfair advantages, and ever since she had been old enough to be aware of them she had shamelessly used them. Staying at the top of the modelling profession was very hard, and working flat-out often wasn't enough; you had to use every one of the assets you had been given. The only other person she knew who was impervious to the way she looked was her father. He was proud of his beautiful daughter, of course, but she had never been able to get her own way with him simply by batting her long eyelashes at him or looking irresistibly pretty.

And she obviously wasn't going to be able to get round Maxim Brenner in that way, either. That was going to make her stay here doubly difficult.

Was she going to stay? Cleo asked herself. Had she finally made that decision? On the other hand, how could she break the very firm promise she had made to her father, *and* let him be cheated out of the money and the portrait?

She gave a small sigh. 'How long will this portrait take?' she asked Maxim.

He shrugged briefly. 'That depends on how co-operative you are.'

'Oh, I'll be *very* co-operative,' she said with some fervour. She would do anything that would make her stay here as short as possible.

A cynical look crossed his face. 'Do you know how to be co-operative?'

'What do you mean by that?'

'You've obviously been spoilt and pampered all your life, you probably only ever do what you want to do. If you've decided that you don't want your portrait painted then we're going to run into endless friction.'

'I'm not like that!' Cleo denied at once. 'And I *do* want this portrait painted. I promised my father that I'd go through with it, and I don't break my promises.'

'You came very close a little while ago, when you were ready to walk out,' Maxim pointed out coolly.

'That was because I didn't expect you to behave in such an uncivilised way!'

His dark eyes gleamed. 'Stay around, and you might run into a few more things that you didn't expect.'

'What kind of things?' Cleo said warily.

'We might as well get a few points straight from the very beginning. I'm not interested in painting your portrait, I simply agreed to it because your father offered such a very large sum of money. Yes, you're beautiful, with those startling eyes and that pale gold hair, but I've never been interested in trying to capture beauty on canvas; after a while all that perfection simply becomes boring. I like to paint people with character, experience, people who've lived hard lives, fascinating lives, dangerous or difficult lives. Prettiness is something that soon fades, but character is something that lasts a lifetime.'

'And you think that I don't have character?' said Cleo indignantly.

Maxim shrugged. 'How can you, when you've been looked after by a rich father for the whole of your life? You've never had to strive or struggle for anything; my guess is that he's always bought you everything you've ever wanted, sheltered you from the outside world and any unpleasantness that's ever threatened you. Even now, when you're not modelling you still live at home with him, you rely on his money, his protection. They're a shield against real life and all its harshness. You're what—twenty-two, twenty-three?—and yet you haven't even started to grow up yet. No, Cleo, I don't think you have character.'

And with that damning indictment he turned and walked out of the kitchen, leaving her too shaken to deny what he had just said, or indeed to say anything at all.

CHAPTER TWO

FOR some time, Cleo just stood in the middle of the kitchen, forgetting how wet she was, not thinking about anything except those last words Maxim had thrown at her. He couldn't possibly be right, she told herself over and over. She *did* have character, she wasn't just the horribly spoilt daughter of a rich father. She had her own career, and she had worked very hard at it; she was now one of the top models in the country. How many other girls could claim that?

And would she have been able to claim it, if her father hadn't opened so many doors for her when she was first starting out? asked a traitorous little voice inside her head? Yes—she had the looks, the tall, elegant body; she probably would eventually have been able to make it on her own. But it had been her father's money that had paid for the perfect grooming, and her first portfolio of superbly professional photographs. He had been able to introduce her to and get her noticed by the right people. And she even suspected, although he had never admitted it, that he had had a hand in her signing with one of the top model agencies. His business activities were so extensive that even she didn't know quite how far his influence extended.

Cleo shook her head with sudden impatience. She didn't want to think about that right now. In fact, it was something she had successfully managed to push right to the back of her mind for a very long time.

She would ignore everything that Maxim had said to her, she told herself firmly. Anyway, what business was it of his? He was going to paint her portrait, and that was all. Her private life, her secret worries and misgivings, were absolutely nothing to do with him.

She wriggled out of her wet cotton jacket and decided that her first priority was to find her room and change into some dry clothes. She had no idea where Maxim had gone, but it was typical of the man to disappear without even bothering to show her to her room. And he had the nerve to accuse *her* of having no manners!

Cleo decided to go and find him. There was no point in wandering around this big house on her own, getting completely lost. She supposed he had gone back to the room where he had first taken her—and told her to take her clothes off! Now that she had time to think about it, she realised that it had been converted to a kind of studio, with canvases propped against the chairs and what must have been paints piled up on the table.

The only trouble was, there were several doors leading off the hallway beyond the kitchen, and she couldn't remember which one Maxim had propelled her through. She opened the first door, and found herself looking into a sitting-room. It had large, comfortable chairs, small tables scattered around rather haphazardly and piled with books and magazines, and a big window which looked out on to the rain-soaked, wildly overgrown garden. The second door led into a room which had a television, video and music centre. Tapes, books and cassettes filled the shelves which lined the walls, and there was a huge couch with fat cushions, where you could sprawl out in comfort as you read, listened to music or watched a video. There were pale but warm colours on the walls and ceilings, and thick plain carpets beneath her feet.

Cleo realised, with some surprise, that the interior of this house had been designed with comfort in mind, and that the air of casual disorder added to the relaxed atmosphere. It was a complete contrast to the rather stark exterior. And it was *very* different from her own home, where everything was immaculate and elegant. The furniture had thin, finely carved legs and was polished every day, so that it glowed richly; the carpets were delicately patterned, and the ceilings were covered with intricately designed plasterwork.

Yet she had to admit that, against all expectations, Maxim Brenner's house was somehow more homely. Of course, she hadn't seen all of it yet, but she supposed the rest of the rooms followed the same design. It was the kind of house where you wouldn't be afraid to put a cup down on one of the tables in case you marked the pristine surface, where you would feel free to flop down on to one of the large couches and put your feet up, or walk around barefoot on the soft, thick carpets.

Of course, I prefer my own home, Cleo told herself firmly. How could she not prefer her father's house, with its beautiful furniture and paintings, each room individually designed with exquisite taste?

She pushed open the next door, and finally found herself in the room she had been in earlier. She gave a sigh of relief. Once Maxim had shown her to her bedroom, she would be able to get out of these wet clothes. Then she would ring her father, to let him know that she had arrived safely. And she might have a few comments to make on his choice of a portrait painter!

Cleo walked further into the room, but then stopped dead. Maxim was standing at the far end, where a large couch had been pushed under the big picture window.

There was a naked girl now stretched out on the couch. And Maxim had his fingers lightly linked around her leg!

''W-what are you doing?' Cleo spluttered.

Maxim glanced round, looking quite unconcerned. 'I thought you'd be in your room unpacking by now.'

'Obviously! But you forgot to tell me where my room is.'

'You're staying in the annexe. Go to the end of the hall, turn right and go through the second door,' he said concisely.

Cleo began to back towards the door, feeling highly embarrassed, and very annoyed with herself for feeling that way. After all, *she* hadn't done anything to feel embarrassed about!

The girl on the couch turned her head and smiled at Cleo. 'Don't feel awkward about seeing me like this, it happens all the time, it really doesn't worry me at all,' she said in a friendly voice.

'Don't move your head,' ordered Maxim. 'And if you could bend your leg a little——' His fingers circled the girl's calf again, shifting her leg to a different position. 'Is that comfortable?' he asked.

'As long as I don't have to hold this pose for too long,' the girl said to him.

Cleo audibly let out her breath. 'You're the life model,' she said, with just a touch of relief. 'Mr Brenner is going to paint you.'

'Today I'm just going to do a few preliminary sketches,' said Maxim, stepping back from the couch and giving a small frown as he studied the pose the girl was now holding. 'The light's too bad to paint.' Then he looked at Cleo. 'If you looked more like this, instead of having barely enough flesh on you to hold your bones together, then I might be interested in doing a nude study of you. This is the kind of body I like, solid and earthy, with plenty of curves and texture, strong arms and legs, a well-rounded backside——'

'A body with character?' Cleo cut in with just a touch of sarcasm.

'Exactly,' Maxim agreed. 'It's a body that's been used and lived-in; it's a long way from perfect but that's what makes it interesting.'

'Hey,' said the girl with a grin, 'there's a person inside this lived-in body, and she would like to hear some *nice* things said about her.'

'I am saying nice things about you,' Maxim told her with an answering smile.

'He doesn't like perfection,' Cleo said, still with a hint of sarcasm. 'He thinks it's boring.' Then she turned back to Maxim. 'I'm going to find my rooms, and then unpack. I'll leave you to get on with your—work.'

She managed to put a great deal of meaning into that last word. She saw his dark eyes flicker warningly, but she was already on her way out of the door. Quite suddenly she wanted to get away from that room with the naked girl and the tall, dark man. For some reason, something about it disturbed her. She wasn't a prude, of course she wasn't. But there had been an unexpectedly sensual undertone to that little scene that had made her feel slightly hot and bothered.

Cleo followed Maxim's directions and easily found her way to the annexe. Although it didn't have a kitchen, it was otherwise self-contained, with a sitting-room, bathroom, and a large bedroom with a double bed, loads of cupboard and wardrobe space, and a comfortable armchair by the window. She was just about to strip off her wet clothes when she realised that her suitcase was still out in the car. With a small groan she trekked out to fetch it, and then puffed her way back to the annexe again, hauling the heavy case and a couple of smaller bags.

She finally wriggled out of her wet things and put on a soft, comfortable sweatshirt with matching jogging trousers. Then she spent quite some time carefully putting away the rest of her clothes. She had brought quite a selection with her, since she hadn't been able to decide what to wear for the portrait. She had a couple of formal dresses, elegant skirts and silk blouses, designer sports wear, beautifully cut jeans and skin tight Lycra tops. Out of all that, she ought to be able to find *something* suitable for her portrait, she told herself wryly.

She dried and restyled her still damp hair, so that it hung in glossy curls to her shoulders. Then she decided to go and ring her father. He would worry about her until she let him know that she had arrived safely.

There was a phone outside in the hall. Cleo quickly dialled the number, and her father answered almost straight away.

'Hello, Dad,' she said. 'I'm just ringing to let you know that I'm here.'

'Did you have a good journey?'

'Yes, it was fine, apart from the pouring rain. And it's *still* pouring with rain,' she said with an exaggerated sigh.

'I'm sure that the weather will improve,' her father said briskly. 'What's Maxim Brenner like?'

'You already know, don't you?' Cleo said in surprise. 'I mean, you have met him.'

'No, we've only spoken on the phone. I couldn't spare the time to travel up to Cumbria, and he was too busy to come down to London, to meet up with me.'

'You've only spoken to him on the phone?' repeated Cleo with rising indignation. 'Do you mean to say that you sent me to stay with someone you'd never even met?'

'Maxim Brenner was recommended by a close friend of mine. Mr Brenner has already painted portraits of my friend's two daughters; they both stayed at his house until the portraits were finished and neither of them encountered any problems. I spoke to Mr Brenner extensively on the phone, and then I had someone make some further checks. It seems that clients often stay at his house when they're having portraits painted, and there's never been any hint of trouble or scandal. You'll be perfectly safe over the next few days.'

'I still think that you should have told me this before. Or at least have travelled up here with me.'

'You're twenty-three years old, Cleo,' said her father, and she thought that she could hear an uncharacteristic tinge of weariness in his voice. 'I think that's old enough to cope with a simple situation like this. Anyway, Maxim Brenner has an international reputation. He's hardly likely to risk ruining it by jumping on you the moment you walk through the door.'

Cleo blinked. Her father had never spoken to her quite like that before. What was wrong?

'Is something the matter?' she asked with a small frown.

'No—no, of course not,' he said after a short pause.

She gave a small sigh of relief. Her father would never lie to her. He had probably just had a bad day at work.

'I really don't like it here,' she told him, getting back to her own problems. 'Maxim Brenner isn't at all the way I expected him to be. In fact, he isn't even a gentleman!'

'What has he done? Or not done?' asked her father a little drily.

Cleo was just about to blurt out the story of how he had locked her out in the rain, but then stopped herself. She didn't think that she wanted to tell her father about that, right now. Instead, she tried to think of some other derogatory thing to say about Maxim Brenner.

'He hasn't done one thing to try and make me feel at home here,' she complained at last. 'And he didn't even carry in my case for me, although it was very heavy, and it was pouring with rain!'

'Perhaps he was wrapped up in his work,' suggested her father.

'Are you making excuses for him?'

'I'm just saying that you can't always expect people to abandon whatever they're doing so that they can run around waiting on you, Cleo.'

There it was again, that rather tired note in his voice, as if he were really only half listening to her.

But there was a lot more that Cleo wanted to say, and she was determined that he would take notice. 'He had a naked woman here this afternoon,' she announced. That was sure to shock her father, she thought with some satisfaction. Perhaps it would even be enough to make him say that she was to come home at once, never mind about the portrait, he didn't want her staying in Maxim Brenner's house one moment longer if that kind of thing went on under his roof.

Instead, though, her father reacted with total indifference. 'You have to expect that kind of thing if you're staying with a painter. Most of them use life models at some time or the other. Anyway, why does that bother you, Cleo? When you're modelling, you often share changing-rooms with the other girls. You all strip off together when you're changing into the next set of clothes; you must see half-naked women all the time.'

That was true, of course. Cleo hadn't expected her father to take that point of view, though. And she certainly hadn't expected this total lack of sympathy!

'Look, I've got to go now,' he went on, 'I've several very important calls to make. Give me a ring when the portrait's finished and you're ready to come home.'

'Oh, I'll phone you before then,' she said at once. 'After all, the portrait may take several days, and you'll want to know how it's going.'

'Yes—all right,' said her father, after a short pause. 'Goodbye, Cleo.'

She began to say goodbye, but he had already hung up, as if he were in a hurry to go somewhere. Cleo gave a small puzzled frown. Something wasn't right. She wondered if she should phone him back and ask again if anything was the matter, but then decided against it. He was probably only over-tired; he always worked much too hard. She would ring him again in a couple of days, she was sure he would be back to his usual self by then.

Realising that she hadn't had anything to eat since a couple of sandwiches at a motorway service station this morning, she made her way to the kitchen. Although it was still very early in the evening, the overcast sky made it so gloomy that she had to switch the lights on. Immediately the kitchen looked a much cheerier place. Copper saucepans gleamed as they hung from their hooks, rich red quarry tiles covered the floor, and there were larger, hand painted tiles on the walls, with designs of exotic birds and flowers in vivid colours.

There was no sign of any dinner, though. Cleo looked around with disappointment. She had hoped to find saucepans bubbling on the stove, or mouthwatering aromas wafting out of the oven.

Just then, the door opened and Maxim walked in. Cleo turned and looked at him, then raised one perfectly shaped blonde eyebrow.

'No naked model in tow?' she asked pointedly.

'Lizzie's gone home,' he said equably.

'I didn't hear a car leave.'

'That's because she came on her bike.'

'You let her cycle home in this pouring rain?' Cleo said in disbelief.

'Unlike you, she came fully prepared for the weather. She had a waterproof mac and trousers, and strong shoes.'

'She certainly wasn't wearing any of them when *I* saw her,' she retorted.

Maxim gave a small growl. 'How much longer are you going to make a big issue of the fact that Lizzie was posing in the nude? Do you have some kind of hang-up about it? What's your problem?'

'I don't have a problem,' Cleo insisted at once. 'It's just that I'm not used to that sort of thing.'

Maxim immediately looked cynical. 'You're a model, aren't you? When you're changing outfits at fashion shows, you must strip off with the other girls. And you probably share dressing-rooms on photographic assignments. Naked girls can't be exactly a novelty, in your line of work.'

It was virtually the same thing that her father had said, just a short time ago. And it was all the more galling, because Cleo knew that they were right. She didn't even

Cleo was almost speechless. No one had ever spoken to her quite like that before!

'Modelling certainly isn't an easy option,' she told him fiercely, finally finding her voice again. 'I've just come back from a week in Bermuda, where I had to stand for long hours in the sun every day before they could finally get the photographs they wanted. And before that I was in America for nearly a month, travelling around all over the place, hardly ever staying in the same hotel for more than a couple of nights.'

'It must have been totally exhausting,' drawled Maxim.

'It was!' she said, infuriated by his cynical attitude.

'More tiring than serving in a shop, standing on your feet all day and every day? Or working at a word processor in an office, staring at a small flickering screen for hour after hour? And the shopgirls, the typists, don't get a chance to travel the world, or get paid outrageous sums of money simply for looking beautiful.'

'It isn't my fault that I look the way I do,' Cleo said defiantly.

'No, it isn't,' he agreed. 'But it would make you a more attractive person if you were more grateful for being given assets and advantages that other girls would give an arm and a leg for.'

'I don't think that I need to try and be more attractive in any way,' she said in a stiff tone.

Maxim's dark eyebrows lifted sceptically. 'You think you have the perfect personality to go with that perfect face and perfect body?'

'Stop twisting my words,' Cleo retorted with some annoyance. 'I know very well that I'm not perfect. Even my face has a couple of tiny flaws.'

'Yes, I know,' he said coolly. 'I'd already noticed them.'

She immediately looked at him anxiously, forgetting everything else that had been said. 'You have? You mean they're getting more noticeable?'

'Only to someone who paints faces for a living. Don't panic, I should think it'll be at least another couple of years, maybe longer, before the camera picks them up.'

Cleo still looked worried, though. 'A couple of years,' she reflected. 'That's not long.'

'There's always plastic surgery,' Maxim said in an unconcerned voice. 'The right surgeon can keep you looking artificially good for the rest of your life. Of course, he'll stretch your skin until there isn't an ounce of character left in your face, and twenty-year-old breasts never look quite right on a sixty-year-old body. But it can be done.'

Cleo gave a small shudder. 'No, not surgery,' she said, almost in a whisper. 'I'd never have surgery.'

Maxim looked at her more closely, as if something in her tone of voice had alerted him to something. 'Because you're afraid of it?' he said at last.

She didn't answer, and to her relief he didn't take it any further.

'About dinner,' he said, as if suddenly deciding that this was a good time to change the subject. 'When I'm at home, I cook for myself. I eat at odd hours, though, to fit in with my work, so you'd better make your own arrangements about meals. The cupboards are well stocked, so use whatever you need.'

As his words slowly sank in, Cleo lifted her head and looked at him. 'You mean that I've got to cook my own meals?'

Maxim looked back at her rather coolly. 'What did you expect? That I'd cook them for you?'

'Well—no—but I thought—there must be someone who looks after you,' she said with a gathering frown.

'Why? Don't you think I'm old enough to look after myself?'

The faintly mocking tone in his voice made her flush slightly.

'Who keeps the house looking so clean?' she argued.

'Mrs Branson, from the village, comes up two or three times a week to flick away the worst of the dust, hoover the muddy footprints from the carpet, and keep the kitchen and bathrooms from looking too disreputable.'

'Then surely *she* could cook my meals?' Cleo insisted.

'She probably could—but why should she? I only have her in to clean because I simply don't have enough time to do it myself.'

'Perhaps she would do it if I paid her?' she offered. 'I can well afford it, and it would only be for a few days, while I'm staying here.'

Maxim's dark eyes began to harden and the faint lines of amusement disappeared from the corners of his mouth.

'Are you so used to being waited on hand and foot that you're too lazy even to get your own dinner?'

'I'm not lazy,' Cleo denied vehemently. 'But I can't——' She swallowed hard, and stared at the floor so that she wouldn't have to see Maxim's face. 'I can't cook,' she confessed at last.

'Everyone can put a simple meal together,' he said dismissively.

'Well, *I* can't.'

'Why not.'

'Because—well, because I've never had to,' she admitted, trying not to look and sound totally ashamed, and failing on both counts.

'Every meal you've ever had in your life has been prepared and cooked by someone else?' Maxim said slowly, in some disbelief.

'When I'm at home, the housekeeper provides all our meals. And when I'm away, I eat at the hotel or find a nearby restaurant.'

Cleo's face was nearly scarlet by now, because she was well aware that this latest admission was only going to reinforce Maxim's opinion that she was a spoilt rich bitch. Of course, she didn't *care* what this man thought of her, she told herself hurriedly. But she was going down in her own estimation, as well as his, and she didn't like that.

'I don't have to know how to cook, do I?' she added rather defiantly.

'Of course not,' agreed Maxim. 'But don't you think that everyone should be able to look after their own basic needs? Or are you so used to paying for what you want that you don't even try to be independent?'

'I *am* independent,' Cleo insisted at once. 'I've a job—a very well paid job—my own circle of friends, and a good social life.'

'But you're still living at home with Daddy,' Maxim pointed out, and there was a definite scathing note in his voice this time.

'Why not?' she challenged him. 'I love my father, and I get on well with him.'

'You don't have to stop loving him. But it's certainly time you were independent of him. It takes guts to stand on your own two feet, though,' he went on, his dark eyes boring into her. 'Perhaps you just don't have what it takes.'

'That's easy for you to say. You're a man. It's different for men!'

'It's no different at all. And before you begin to accuse me of not understanding, let me tell you right now that I understand perfectly. I had a powerful, domineering father, as well. I know exactly how hard it is to break free of that kind of influence.'

'My father isn't domineering,' Cleo said loyally.

'Are you saying that you have a healthy relationship with him? That he doesn't have too much influence over your life?'

'Yes!'

'Then why are you here?' Maxim challenged her.

She blinked. 'What do you mean?'

'Why are you staying here, in my house?'

'To have my portrait painted, of course.'

'And do you *want* to have your portrait painted?'

'No, I don't,' she said without thinking. Then she realised what she had admitted, and went bright red all over again.

'You're here because it's what your father wants,' Maxim told her coolly. 'You're doing what he wants, instead of what you want.'

'You don't understand——' she began. Then she shut up again. She didn't want to explain about her mother; about the two portraits that were going to hang side by side.

'I think I understand very well,' Maxim said, fixing that dark gaze on her again. 'It's the easy way out, isn't it, to stay a child? Loved and protected by a powerful father? But one day, you're going to have to start growing up, Cleo. And the longer you leave it, the harder it's going to be for you. If I were you, I'd make a start on it very soon.'

Cleo lifted her head high and tossed back her pale blonde hair. 'Thank you, but I don't need a lecture on how to run my life,' she told him. 'Just as I don't need to learn how to cook. Forget about dinner, I'll go out later and find a restaurant.'

'Using money to solve your problems again?' he goaded her softly.

'I don't have any problems,' she retorted. 'At least, I didn't until I came here and met you!'

Maxim merely smiled; not a friendly smile, more a mocking curve of his lips.

'I certainly wouldn't want to be a problem, so I'll get back to work and leave you on your own. Remember what I've said, though, Cleo. If you go on like this for the rest of your life, it isn't going to *be* much of a life.'

After he had gone, she sat and glowered darkly for a while. How dared he say all those things to her? And how did he know so much about her? she suddenly wondered with a fresh frown. Had he been asking about her, prying into her private life? That was something that she definitely intended to follow up. But not now—in the morning.

Cleo knew that she had had as much of Maxim Brenner as she could handle in one day.

CHAPTER THREE

BECAUSE the rain was still bucketing down outside, Cleo decided to forget about any plans she might have had for going out to find a local restaurant. Instead, she made herself a pile of sandwiches, and finished her rather uninspiring meal with some fresh fruit and a cup of coffee. Luckily, she rarely had to worry about her weight. She could eat almost anything she liked without putting on more than an extra couple of pounds. And, since she wasn't working again until the end of the month, there would be plenty of time to get herself back into perfect shape if she went slightly over her limit.

By the time she had cleared away the dishes it was dark and she was yawning hard. Time to tumble into bed, she decided. It had been a *very* long day.

She slept well, and when she woke up in the morning the bedroom seemed surprisingly bright. It was a couple of minutes before Cleo sleepily realised what was causing the brightness. The sun was shining!

She got up, padded over to the window and pulled the curtains. Outside, the sky was a clear blue, the sun shone down warmly, and birds were singing happily in the nearby trees.

'Maxim said the sun would be shining this morning,' she said to herself in surprise. Then she wrinkled her nose. 'I bet he's one of those men who's always right about everything!'

After a quick shower, she spent some time going through the clothes she had brought with her. There was a good chance that Maxim was going to start work on her portrait today, so she had better decide what she was going to wear.

Half an hour later, Cleo had tried on practically everything she had brought with her, and still not made up her mind. In the end, she decided she had better play safe and settle for a plain black dress. It made a startling contrast to her pale blonde hair and green eyes, and she could jazz it up with some jewellery if Maxim thought it was too plain.

The dress was slinky and sophisticated, and clung tightly to every curve of her body. Cleo brushed her cheekbones with blusher to accentuate them, whisked gold shadow on to her eyelids to give them an almost feline slant, darkened her lashes with mascara, coloured her lips and then glossed them.

After a long, critical look in the mirror and a final toss of her head so that her blonde curls looked tumbled and casual, she nodded with satisfaction. A good professional job—but, of course, she had been taught by professionals.

Cleo slid her feet into a pair of high-heeled, thin-strapped sandals that helped to show off the long line of her legs, and also her feet, which were well-shaped and surprisingly small and dainty for such a tall girl. Then she left the annexe and went along to the kitchen, to make herself some coffee.

Before she reached it, though, Maxim opened the door of his studio and stood in front of her, blocking her path. His sudden appearance made her jump. Like it or not, the man certainly had presence—and he knew how to make it felt!

'I've some free time this morning,' he said without preamble. 'Let's get down to some work.'

Cleo began to recover a little from the shock of seeing him. 'Well, I'm sorry, but it isn't convenient. I haven't had any breakfast yet,' she informed him.

'Breakfast can wait until later. And you look as if you rarely eat, anyway. Do you exist on mineral water and the odd slimming biscuit, like most models?'

'I eat normal meals,' Cleo said indignantly.

'As long as someone else cooks them for you,' he reminded her mockingly. Then his manner changed and became more efficient. 'If I don't start work on your portrait now, then it'll probably have to wait until tomorrow. That's fine by me, it makes no difference to me how long it takes. But I was under the impression that you wanted to get it finished as quickly as possible.'

She certainly did. Then she could go back to London, and her normal life.

'All right,' Cleo agreed, 'I'll sit for you now. I can always eat later.'

She followed him into the studio, which was lit this morning by the brilliant sunlight which poured in through the huge picture window and looked entirely different from the shadowed room it had been yesterday. A large table held a huge assortment of paints, brushes, knives, bottles of liquid which she supposed were cleaning fluids, and paint-stained rags. Unused canvases were stacked in one corner, while a couple of others stood on easels and seemed to be in a half-finished state.

Cleo walked over to the window, and then blinked. Yesterday, low cloud and rain had obscured the view beyond a couple of yards. This morning, in the clear light, she could see for what seemed like miles. And what a view it was!

From Maxim Brenner's house, emerald-green fields rolled down to a wide stretch of water that glinted in the sunlight. And beyond the water the mountains soared gently up into the blue sky, their rounded peaks making a long, humped line that eventually disappeared into the soft haze in the far distance. The slopes of the mountains were dappled with different shades of green, and criss-crossed with dry-stone walls that climbed up to dizzying heights. Small white specks moved around, revealing themselves as sheep, and overhead a solitary buzzard lazily wheeled, riding the thermals as the sun began to heat up the air.

'An improvement on yesterday?' said Maxim drily, walking over to join her.

'It certainly is! What's that water down there? A river?'

'No, it's a small lake. You can only see the far end of it from here. You'll get a better view if you walk down to the village.'

'I can't see a village,' Cleo said promptly.

Maxim pointed to a thick stand of trees to the left. 'The houses and cottages are hidden by those trees. In winter, when the leaves have fallen, you can see the roofs, and the lights shining from the windows.'

'I'd like to be here in the winter,' she said, without thinking. 'To see the snow on the mountaintops and everything covered with a white glittering frost.'

Maxim looked at her a little sceptically. 'You made enough fuss yesterday about a shower of rain; I really don't think you'd enjoy our winters. It gets very cold, it's often very wet, and the snow doesn't just stay up on the mountaintops, it comes right down into the valleys and piles up everywhere, several feet of it in a bad winter.'

'I could cope with that,' she insisted. 'And that wasn't a shower of rain yesterday,' she added with a small grimace, 'it was an absolute downpour!'

'The locals would probably consider it a shower,' he said equably. 'And now we've finished admiring the view and discussing the weather, perhaps we could get down to some work?'

'All right,' she said. 'What do you want me to do?' She lifted one of her well-shaped eyebrows as she added wryly, 'Pose on that couch?'

'Not unless you're going to insist on taking your clothes off for this portrait,' he said, his dark eyes briefly glinting. 'Try sitting in that chair,' he went on, pointing to a high-backed chair that stood the window. 'Just relax and sit naturally. I'll do a few preliminary sketches, and we'll see how it goes.'

Cleo settled herself into the chair, and felt ridiculously self-conscious. Since she had posed for the camera hundreds, probably thousands of times, she had no idea why she should feel like that. After all, she was only doing something that she did almost every day of her working life.

Maxim simply looked at her for a couple of minutes, an intense and yet impersonal scrutiny, as if he were professionally assessing every inch of her. Cleo had never felt so uncomfortable in her entire life. She also felt strangely hot. She had to force herself to sit still, and not squirm restlessly under that dark gaze.

When he had finally finished studying her, he made no effort to pick up the drawing-pad and pencil that he had put to hand nearby. Instead, he got to his feet.

'This is useless,' he said with a frown.

'What do you mean?'

'You're not sitting, you're posing. There isn't one single thing about you that looks in the least natural, from your painted face to those ridiculous shoes on your feet.'

'There's nothing wrong with my shoes *or* my face,' Cleo retorted. 'I know how to make myself look good, it's how I earn my living.'

'I don't want you looking good, I want you looking *yourself*,' he growled at her.

'This is me!' she said with growing annoyance. 'It's how I look almost every day of my life.'

'No, it's how you make yourself look. It's a glossy image for the camera, a façade. Go and clean off that make up, brush all those lacquered curls out of your hair and take off that dress.'

'What's wrong with my dress?' she demanded.

'It flattens your breasts and shows almost every bone in your body.'

'That's what it's meant to do. It's a very expensive dress, and it's been specially designed to cling tightly all over.'

'Well, it certainly does that,' Maxim drawled, his eyes drifting over her as if he could see right through the thin material to the pale skin underneath. 'But you're too skinny for it to be effective. It makes your breasts virtually disappear, and it probably does the same for your backside. Go and take it off, Cleo. Put on some sensible clothes and find yourself some wellington boots in the cupboard under the stairs.'

'Why?' she said, rather crossly.

'Because we're going out. I need some fresh air, I've been working half the night. You can come with me. We're getting nowhere here, we might as well leave it for a while. Anyway, I'd like to see you in a natural light.

I'm not even going to begin to try to paint you until I find out what lies under all that sophisticated gloss.'

'Perhaps there isn't anyone in the least interesting,' Cleo retorted. 'Maybe you'll find someone who's plain and very ordinary.'

Maxim's eyes immediately narrowed. 'Is that what you're afraid of? That no one will like the person underneath the painted façade?'

'I'm not afraid of anything,' she said at once. She was very well aware that wasn't the truth, though. There were a whole lot of things that scared her. And, just lately, that had included her whole way of life. There were days when it seemed so frighteningly empty. Something about it—perhaps *everything* about it—seemed to be wrong. Things needed to change. Perhaps *she* needed to change. She didn't know how to go about it, though; didn't even know what changes she wanted to make.

There was no way that she was going to admit any of her doubts and fears to this man, though. Nor was she going to let this conversation go any further. She had the feeling that Maxim Brenner was very good at ferreting out people's secrets.

She decided that it might be a good idea to go on that walk, though. It would be something to do, and the fresh air might help to chase away these very unsettling thoughts that she kept getting lately.

'I'll walk down to the village with you,' she told him. 'But I don't need to borrow any wellingtons, I brought some boots with me.'

'We'll be taking a short cut across the fields,' he said. 'And after yesterday's rain, the paths will be pretty muddy. Fancy fashion boots will be useless.'

Cleo was about to argue with him, but then stopped because he was right—again! Her boots were a soft, pale suede, and definitely not designed for tramping across boggy fields.

She went to her room and changed into jeans and a T-shirt. Then she found the cupboard under the stairs and opened the door, to look for the wellingtons.

Her eyebrows shot up as she saw more than a dozen pairs lined up inside, all in different sizes. Maxim must keep a lot of spares, to lend out to visitors! She fished out a pair that looked as they would fit her, then glanced round the cupboard with a small frown. As well as the boots, there was a football, a couple of pairs of roller-skates, a small doll's pram, a scooter and several boxed games piled up haphazardly in the corner. Why so much children's stuff? Then the obvious reason occurred to her. Maxim must paint children's portraits, as well as adults. He kept these things to amuse the children; they would need something to play with in the breaks between sittings.

She pulled on the wellingtons, which were definitely more practical than elegant. Then she went to find Maxim.

He was waiting for her at the front door. They went out into the bright sunshine, and Cleo lifted her face up to the gentle warmth and gave a small sigh of satisfaction.

'Perhaps this place does have its good points, after all,' she said. 'Great views, and just occasionally it stops raining!' Then she looked at Maxim. 'Have you lived here all your life?'

'No,' he said, after a short pause. 'Only for four years.'

'Where did you live before that?'

'In London.'

'What happened?' asked Cleo. 'Did you get tired of the big city lights, and decide to head for the hills?'

'It was—more convenient to live here.'

Her eyebrows shot up. 'More convenient? But surely it's easier to be based in London, if you're a painter?'

'Life does exist outside the capital,' he said shortly. Then he lengthened his stride and easily drew ahead of her, putting an obvious end to the conversation.

Cleo looked at him thoughtfully as she followed him across the field that stretched from the edge of the garden, down towards the lake in the distance. She seemed to have hit a raw nerve. What had happened in London, to make him leave? Something that he obviously still didn't want to talk about!

She was dying to ask more questions, but there was something about the set of his shoulders that was distinctly forbidding. She would try again later, she promised herself. There was a lot more that she wanted to know about Maxim Brenner.

They walked on in silence for quite a while, the grass green and spongy beneath their feet, and sunlight glinting on the water as they drew nearer to the lake. Cleo could see cottages beginning to appear now, their grey roofs appearing behind the trees, and their stone walls looking a little sombre even in the sunlight.

Maxim finally slowed his pace, allowing her to catch up with him. 'There are a couple of small shops in the village,' he told her. 'Between them, they stock most of the basics. If you need anything else, you'll probably have to go into Ambleside or Windermere.'

Cleo gave a small shrug. 'I think that I've brought everything with me that I'll need. And I won't be staying that long—will I?'

'That depends on how the portrait goes. And that, in turn, depends on how co-operative you are.'

'I'll be *very* co-operative,' she assured him at once. 'I told you that before.'

One of his dark eyebrows gently lifted. 'You don't like it here? You don't want to stay any longer than you have to?'

Cleo looked at the clear sky, the bright, rain-washed colours of the lake, the village, and the mountains. 'Oh, I think that I could get to like it here,' she said. 'But my life is back in London.'

'And your life there is so important, so absorbing, that you can't wait to get back to it?'

Was he mocking her again? She couldn't tell, and that annoyed her.

'My work is there,' she said rather stiffly. 'That's certainly important to me.'

'Surely your work takes you all over the world? You could live anywhere, and still carry on modelling. But your father lives in London, doesn't he? And that's what keeps you there, because you're a daddy's girl, aren't you, Cleo?'

His voice had taken on a derogatory tone that made her bristle.

'I don't want another lecture on my relationship with my father!'

'And you're not going to get one,' Maxim said, to her surprise. 'You're old enough, and intelligent enough, to know the truth about it by now. It's your problem if you won't face up to it.'

'It is *not* a problem,' she said furiously.

He merely shrugged and looked totally sceptical, which infuriated her still further. What right did this man have to criticise the way she lived her life?

She gave a fierce scowl, and refused to look at his dark-eyed, oh, so good-looking face. What was she doing here, anyway, going for a morning stroll with him as if they were the closest of friends?

'I'm going back to the house,' she declared.

'Now you're being childish,' Maxim said calmly. 'And childishness isn't a very attractive trait in someone who's twenty-three years old. Instead of throwing a tantrum, why don't you come and look at the lake?'

'I don't throw tantrums!' Cleo said indignantly. 'But I certainly don't intend to stand here while you criticise my father.'

'I'm not criticising your father. We spoke on the phone for some time, and he seemed a very reasonable man. He likes to get his own way, of course—but that could be said of a lot of men, particularly those who are used to wielding power and influence.'

'Including you?'

'Including me,' Maxim agreed, his eyes suddenly gleaming. 'In fact, you should really get on very well with me. I'm very like your father, in a lot of ways.'

'You're not like him at all,' Cleo said at once. 'You're an artist!'

Maxim suddenly relaxed and laughed out loud. Cleo looked at him in astonishment. She had been starting to think he was a man who *never* laughed.

'What's so funny?' she said a little crossly as he went on laughing. She had the suspicion now that he was laughing at *her*.

'Nothing,' he said, still grinning. 'Come on, Cleo, I'll show you the lake.'

He began to walk down a narrow road that turned off to the right. She gave another small scowl at his departing back. Then she began to follow him.

It was only because she had nothing better to do, she told herself. And if he annoyed her one more time, then she was going straight back to the house.

It took them only a few minutes to reach the lake, and when Cleo saw it stretching out in front of her, the glittering water surrounded by the green fields and the backdrop of the mountains, she was glad she hadn't decided to turn back.

There were a few other people walking along the shore, some just strolling, others equipped with walking boots and sticks and striding along purposefully, but they were all some distance away. On the lake itself, half a dozen boats bobbed around, searching for some wind to send them flying across the water, and a couple of youngsters were trying, unsuccessfully, to keep their balance on windsurfing boards.

'This is great,' she said appreciatively. 'So uncommercialised and tranquil.'

'It isn't quite as tranquil as it looks,' Max said drily. 'Some developers have got their hands on a tract of land on the far side of the village. They want to build a hotel and holiday cottages, and bring some tourists to this part of the Lakes.'

'I shouldn't think that's very popular with the locals,' Cleo remarked.

'They don't object to tourists. They bring in income and help to create much-needed jobs. They don't even object to plans for a small hotel, as long as it fits in with the environment. But they argue that, instead of holiday cottages, the developers should build reasonably priced homes for local people. Too many young people have to move away because, when a house around here goes up for sale, it's usually sold at a very inflated price as a holiday home. They simply can't afford to buy, and so they leave.'

'That certainly doesn't seem very fair,' she agreed. 'Will the developers change their plans?'

'It isn't very likely,' Maxim said, with some cynicism. 'There's more profit to be had from holiday cottages, and profit's usually all they're interested in.'

They turned away from the lake, and began to walk back up the lane.

'I'd really like to know just how long it's going to take you to finish my portrait,' Cleo said after a while.

'I haven't even started it yet,' he pointed out.

'That isn't *my* fault,' she said at once. 'I was ready to sit for you this morning. You were the one who didn't want to begin working on it.'

'That's my prerogative. I don't work to order.'

'Well, when *will* you begin the portrait?'

'I've no idea,' he said coolly. 'Whenever I can fit it in.'

'Are you that busy?' she said with some scepticism. 'I mean, exactly what else are you working on at the moment?'

'I've a couple of portraits of local dignitaries that need some finishing details, and one of a major film star that's causing problems because she keeps changing the colour of her hair in between each sitting.'

'That doesn't sound too time-consuming,' Cleo said at once.

'Apart from painting, I have business interests that I have to take care of. And I'm also working on a series of nude studies for an exhibition at the end of the year.'

'Oh, yes,' she muttered, colouring slightly. 'Lizzie on the couch!'

Maxim looked amused. 'She's the last one in the series, the others are all finished, so you won't have to worry about any more naked females running around the house.'

'I certainly *wasn't* worried,' she denied, although not altogether truthfully. 'Anyway, why nudes?' she went on. 'Are you fed up with portraits?'

'I never get fed up with portraits. Every human face is quite unique, and there's always the added challenge of trying to capture the character underneath.'

'You'll have a problem with me,' she reminded him a little tartly. 'According to you, I don't *have* a character!'

Maxim merely raised one eyebrow. Then he gave a sudden and unexpectedly wicked grin. 'Are you really interested in knowing why I'm painting nudes?'

'Perhaps you just like naked female bodies,' Cleo suggested drily.

His eyes glinted. 'Most men like naked female bodies. But the reason I like to paint them is quite different. Mostly it's got to do with the texture and colour of skin; it's such fascinating stuff, it changes with age, with the light, even with people's moods. It's one of the most difficult things to paint and get right because you have to put life into it, make it almost breathe. And I like the shape of bodies—all bodies, not just the slim and beautiful ones. The curve of a back, the graceful line of an arm, the powerful set of shoulders and the sensual swell of buttocks—they never stop being fascinating, I could look at them, paint them, until I'm too tired to hold a brush.'

Cleo's green eyes remained locked on his face while he was speaking, transfixed by the emotion and sudden passion in his voice. She didn't think she had ever heard anyone speak with such intensity and commitment. This was a man who clearly loved his work. And she suddenly found herself wondering if he was capable of loving a person with that same passionate intensity.

She suddenly shivered, despite the sunshine, because just the thought of so much raw, unbridled emotion frightened her. She always shied away from anything so uncontrollable. Anyway, what on earth had made her think something like that? Unnerved and unsettled, she began to walk much faster.

'If you've so much work to get through, you probably want to get on with it,' she said rather rapidly. And she kept walking very quickly, with her back to him, all the way back to the house.

When they finally reached it, Maxim shot one quick look at her, his dark brows drawn thoughtfully together. To her relief, though, he didn't say anything. Instead, he let his dark, intense gaze fix on her face for a couple more seconds, then he strode off in the direction of his studio. Cleo kicked off her wellington boots and more slowly made her way into the annexe.

For some reason that she couldn't quite understand, her nerves felt very twitchy. She couldn't sit still, couldn't seem to settle to anything. In the end, she wriggled out of her jeans and T-shirt, pulled on her favourite old leotard that she used when she exercised, and slid a tape of dance music into her personal stereo.

Cleo wasn't a keep-fit fanatic, but she exercised for a short time each day, partly to keep her body supple and in shape for modelling, but mainly because she enjoyed it and found it relaxing. She did simple stretch exercises to music, sometimes breaking into a more vigorous work out when she was feeling particularly energetic.

She clipped the walkman to her waist, fitted the headphones into her ears, and then began to warm up, gradually moving faster and stretching further as she got more involved in the familiar routine. Her pale blonde hair swirled around her face, her breathing got quicker, and the music pounded in her ears, a heavy, sensual beat that made her hips swing provocatively and her body twist and turn with supple abandon.

It wasn't until she spun round in a pirouetting exercise that she saw Maxim standing in the doorway. Cleo stopped dead. Then she ripped the headphones out of her ears and stared at him coldly.

'How long have you been standing there?' she demanded.

'Only a couple of minutes. I knocked, but you didn't hear me.'

'You could have gone away again!'

'But I wanted to watch you.' His dark eyes moved slowly over her body, and then back to her face again. 'This is how I would like to paint you, Cleo,' he went on more softly. 'Your face flushed, your hair damp and tangled. You look relaxed, glowing—as if you've just got out of bed.'

For some reason, his words made her swallow very hard. Then she managed to get some control over herself again.

'I'm afraid that isn't the kind of portrait my father wants,' she said stiffly.

'Of course not,' agreed Maxim. 'He wants a chocolate box picture, with you sitting primly in a chair wearing a pretty dress. Not looking as if you've just left your lover.'

'I haven't got a lover,' she burst out. Then she almost stamped her foot in frustration. Why had she said that?

Maxim didn't look in the least ruffled, though. Or surprised.

'Do you want to tell me why you haven't got a lover, Cleo?' he said at last. 'Does your father want to keep you his little girl for the rest of your life?'

'The decision is mine,' she said furiously. 'And stop talking about my father like that. You're making him sound sick, and he isn't!'

'Then perhaps you're the one with the hang-ups,' Maxim said in the same thoughtful tone. 'You're the one who doesn't want to grow up.'

'Does jumping into bed with someone make you grown-up?' she challenged him.

'No. But running away from all the things that make up an adult life is rather childish.'

'I've had enough of this conversation,' Cleo said heatedly. 'Please get out of here. I want to finish my exercises.'

'I'd rather stay.'

She glared at him. 'Well, you can't!'

His dark eyes glimmered with amusement. 'I'm not being voyeuristic. I want to sketch you while you exercise.'

'I don't want you to do that,' she said at once.

'Why not?'

'Because——' She tried to think of a convincing reason, and was annoyed when she couldn't come up with one. 'I just don't,' she muttered at last.

Instead of going away, though, Maxim came a little further into the room.

'What I'd really like to do is include you in my series of nude studies,' he told her, his eyes fixing on her levelly.

'What?' she yelped. Then she shook her head so vigorously that her blonde hair flew out in all directions. 'No. Definitely no!'

'Don't you like your own body?'

'My body is fine—but that doesn't mean that I want everyone to stare at a nude painting of it,' she retorted.

'Anyway, you said yesterday that you *didn't* want to paint my body, it was too skinny and not interesting enough.'

'I didn't look at you properly yesterday. Anyway, you look different today. No longer cool and sophisticated. You're hot and dishevelled, rather sweaty, much more relaxed, some of your defences are down. I like that,' Maxim said, looking directly into her green eyes. 'I like being able to get behind people's defences.'

Cleo suddenly knew that the scariest thing she could think of was being reduced to a defenceless state by this man.

'I am *not* going to let you do a nude painting of me,' she repeated with absolute determination.

'But I don't want to paint you naked,' Maxim said, throwing her off balance all over again. 'I want to paint you exactly the way you are right now, with that damp leotard clinging to your body, showing all the clear, supple lines, revealing everything without actually showing an inch of flesh. It would be a challenge, to make people see the body underneath the clothing, to make them see it so clearly that they forget the leotard is even there. It would be technically difficult, a nude that isn't nude. But I can do it.'

That passionate intensity was back in his voice again, now. Was it only there when he talked about his work? Cleo wondered. Didn't anything else ever spark off that powerful surge of emotion and adrenalin that lit his dark eyes until they blazed, brought vivid life to his face and an almost sexual tension to his body?

For a few moments, she was almost swept along by his overwhelming forcefulness, she found herself incredibly tempted to say yes, she *would* do it. Just in time, she stopped herself. What would her father say, her friends say, when they saw such a painting? They were used to seeing photographs of her in magazines, often wearing quite skimpy clothes, but this would be different, *very* different. Cleo was quite sure that Maxim Brenner's painting would show her in a way that no one had ever seen her before!

'You were commissioned to do a portrait of me, and that's all I require you to do,' she told him in a stilted, formal voice. 'I don't want to take my clothes off for you, and I don't want any more talk about getting "behind my defences". All you have to do is produce a simple, straightforward painting.'

Maxim's dark eyes locked on to her face again. 'I don't do simple, straightforward paintings. And you are going to strip bare for me, Cleo. Oh, I don't mean literally,' he added, as he saw the sudden flash of alarm on her face. 'I mean that, one way or another, you're eventually going to show me a little of your soul. And *that's* what I'm going to put into your portrait.'

Having delivered that message in a level and yet forceful voice, he turned round and left the room.

CHAPTER FOUR

BY THE time Cleo had stripped off her damp leotard, showered, pulled on a short dress in shocking pink and curled her hair with a hot brush, she felt slightly better. She looked—and felt—more like her old self. And no matter what Maxim Brenner said, she was absolutely determined that her portrait would turn out the way *she* wanted it to look.

A faint rumbling from her stomach reminded her that she hadn't had a proper meal since she had arrived at this house. Cleo picked up the car keys, intending to drive into Ambleside to look for a restaurant. Then she tossed them to one side again, wrinkling her nose. She couldn't be bothered to tackle the narrow, winding roads. Anyway, she wanted something to eat right now.

She went to the kitchen, pulled open the door of the freezer, and then began to rummage through the contents. If she was going to learn to cook, then she had better start with something easy, she decided. And, since all the frozen foods had clear cooking instructions printed on the back, this was a good place to begin.

Then Cleo spied a couple of complete frozen meals, shoved to the back of the freezer. She pulled one out, and found she only had to put it in the oven for half an hour.

'Great,' she said with enthusiasm. 'I'll tackle something more difficult tomorrow.'

While she was waiting for her lunch to cook, she looked through some of the other cupboards. She soon found that Maxim had a good store of fresh food and vegetables, and there was a pile of recipe books stacked on a shelf in the corner. Cleo took a couple down and flicked through them. The instructions seemed easy to follow and her confidence grew. There really didn't seem to be anything to this cooking business, as long as you took it step by step. As she was obviously going to have quite a lot of free time on her hands over the next few days, this would be a good opportunity to have a go at it. Much as she hated to admit it, Maxim had been right, it *was* rather shameful not to be able to cook a meal for herself at her age.

The frozen dinner turned out to be not exactly up to gourmet standard, but Cleo was too hungry to care. She ate every scrap of it, and then finished her meal with fresh fruit.

It was early afternoon by now, and there was no sign of Maxim. She supposed he was in his studio, working on one of his other paintings. Cleo gave a small sigh. It didn't look as if there would be any significant progress on her portrait today. She could see her stay here stretching on indefinitely!

The sunshine outside looked tempting, and she decided that she might as well spend a couple of hours in the garden, relaxing and sunbathing. Although it was early autumn, it was still very warm when the weather was good, and it would be a chance to top up the light golden tan she had got in Bermuda. Cleo changed into shorts and a sleeveless T-shirt, then remembered seeing a couple of folding deckchairs in the cupboard under the stairs, along with the toys and wellington boots. She hauled one out, lugged it out into the garden, and then settled down into it.

Lulled into total relaxation by the sun, the gentle hum of nearby bees and the sound of distant birdsong, she closed her eyes and dozed. It really was very nice here, she told herself, sleepily surfacing again half an hour later. After the constant noise and bustle of central London, it was so quiet, so marvellously peaceful...

An ear-piercing yell from just a few yards away made every nerve in her body jump violently and her eyes fly wide open. Then a second blood-curdling yell followed, and Cleo turned her head just in time to see a small boy rush down towards the bottom of the garden, brandishing something in his hand.

'Give that back!' screeched another voice, and another child hurtled by. A girl this time, Cleo thought, because this one had long, dark hair. Otherwise, it would have been difficult to tell because they were both dressed in well worn jeans and old T-shirts.

The two children tore round the garden, both yelling at the tops of their voices, charging across the overgrown flowerbeds and trampling down the long grass. So much for the peace and quiet! Cleo thought grimly as she got to her feet. And who *were* these children? A couple of local kids, she supposed, probably from the village. They must have come up here because the overgrown garden made a perfect playground. As far as she was concerned, though, they could go straight back to the village. Let them go and disturb someone else's peaceful afternoon!

As the children ran past her, taking absolutely no notice of her, Cleo shot out her hands and gripped hold of their T-shirts, bringing them both to an abrupt halt.

Two pairs of dark eyes slewed round to fix on her face. The children's faces were flushed from their wild running, and they were panting, but Cleo knew that they would quickly recover. She had to march them out of the garden right now, before they wriggled free and raced off again.

'This is private property,' she told them sternly. 'You shouldn't be running around making all that noise. In fact, you'll have to leave.'

They both gaped at her, as if she were speaking nonsense. Cleo tightened her grip on their T-shirts, to stop them bolting. Then she looked at them even more severely. 'Don't pretend to be a couple of little idiots, you understand very well what I'm saying. Now, start walking. You're going straight back home.'

She swung them round, and as she did so, she saw Maxim striding into the garden. She was about to explain that she was ejecting a couple of very young intruders when she saw his face.

Cleo didn't think that she had never seen anyone look so intensely angry. The words she had been about to say dried up in her throat and she felt her knees begin to shake.

'Let go of those children!' Maxim roared at her.

'But—but they were running round your garden, yelling at the tops of their voices and trampling over everything,' she stammered.

'Of course they were. They live here, they're *my* children. Get your hands off them—right now!'

Cleo didn't think she had ever moved more quickly in her life. She let go of them as if they had suddenly turned red hot.

'Your—your children?' she managed to croak.

'William, Alice, go into the house and help your Aunt Sarah to unpack your things,' their father ordered.

They trotted off into the house at once, pausing only to shoot a baleful look at Cleo as they passed her. When they had disappeared from sight, Cleo moved nervously from one foot to the other.

'I—er—I didn't know you had any children,' she muttered at last. 'You never said—nobody told me——'

'There was no reason for you to know,' Maxim said crisply. 'I expected them to be away until the end of the week, they were on holiday with my sister and her family. One of her boys has developed chickenpox, though, so they've all come back early.'

'I'm sorry about what happened, I thought they were children from the village——'

'Even if they had been, there was no need to treat them like young criminals,' Maxim cut in, his eyes darkening again.

'I only grabbed hold of their T-shirts,' Cleo said defensively. 'Anyway, I'd been dozing in the deckchair; I was still half asleep. I didn't have time to think what I was doing.'

'With young children, you have to *make* time to think what you're doing,' he said tersely.

'I'll try and remember that in the future,' she mumbled. 'And I really am sorry.'

'I suppose that there's no permanent harm done,' he conceded. 'Although you've certainly got off on the wrong foot with William and Alice; you're going to find it difficult to make them like you after this.'

Cleo gave a resigned shrug. 'It probably would have been difficult, anyway. I don't know anything about children, I don't know what to say to them, or how to treat them.'

Maxim's eyes narrowed. 'You don't have any young children in your family? No brother, sisters, cousins?'

'None,' Cleo admitted a little sadly. 'There's just me and my father, a couple of elderly aunts, and some grandparents in Australia, although I've only met them once. They went there years ago, to join their son who had emigrated out there. He died soon after they arrived, but they liked it out there so much that they stayed on.'

'Is that why you cling to your father? Because there's no one else?'

'I don't cling!' she denied, although not very truthfully.

Maxim shrugged. 'You certainly don't lead your own life. I intend to make sure that never happens to William and Alice. As soon as they're old enough, they're going to be independent.'

'Don't be surprised if that doesn't happen,' Cleo retorted. 'The one thing you can be certain about is that life never turns out the way you expect!'

He looked at her with rather disconcerting intensity. 'You're disappointed with your life?'

Cleo nearly blurted out that she was disappointed with everything—including herself. Just in time, she bit back the words.

'What could I have to be disappointed about?' she asked instead. 'I'm the girl with everything, aren't I? The great career, the money, the looks—my life is just perfect.' She lifted her head and tossed her hair back defiantly. 'Come on, you'd better introduce me properly to your children, and try to convince them that I'm not some kind of ogre.'

She began to walk quickly towards the house, and didn't see the thoughtful look that Maxim gave her as he followed.

Inside, there was no sign of the children, but there was a dark-haired, dark-eyed woman in her thirties making coffee in the kitchen.

'Oh—this is my sister, Sarah,' Maxim said, almost absently. 'Sarah, this is Cleo. I'm painting her portrait. No coffee for me yet,' he added, as she began to set out an extra cup. 'I'd better go up and make sure that they're unpacking, instead of wrecking the bedrooms!'

He disappeared out the door, and Cleo gave a confused shake of her head.

'This is a bit much to take in,' she said rather helplessly. 'This morning, I thought Maxim was a man living on his own. Now, it turns out he's got two children, a sister, and probably a dozen more relatives that I don't even know about yet!'

His sister gave Cleo a friendly smile. 'I'm afraid that Maxim doesn't give out very much personal information. In fact, he doesn't give out *any*,' she added wryly.

'Is there anyone else I haven't met yet?' Cleo asked rather more hesitantly. 'Like—a wife?'

'His wife died four years ago,' Sarah told her.

'His wife died?' Cleo repeated, shocked. Then she remembered that Maxim had told her he had moved here from London four years ago. That must have been just after it had happened. 'It's always awful when you lose someone close to you,' she said, still shaken. 'It must have hit him very hard.'

'It knocked us all completely off balance for a while,' said his sister. 'Although Maxim and Vivienne—his wife—weren't too close by then. Their marriage—it didn't work out too well.' Then she gave a small shake of her head. 'I probably shouldn't have told you that. Maxim likes to keep his private life *very* private.'

'I know,' said Cleo with some feeling. 'He didn't even tell me he had two children!'

Sarah gave a sudden grin, which made her look disconcertingly like her brother for an instant. 'It must have been quite a shock when William and Alice suddenly turned up out of nowhere. It really was very naughty of Maxim not to tell you about them.'

'I don't think he expected me to meet them,' Cleo said. 'You were all meant to be on holiday until the beginning of next week, and I think he was hoping to finish my portrait and get rid of me by then.'

'Oh, I'm sure that he isn't that eager to get rid of you. Maxim likes beautiful women,' said his sister cheerfully.

Cleo's eyebrows shot up! 'He does? But he keeps telling me that he only likes to paint people with interesting faces, people with lots of character.'

'I'm sure that you're interesting *and* full of character,' said Sarah. 'But I wasn't talking about the women he likes to paint,' she went on, with a mischievous smile.

'Oh,' said Cleo, startled. 'You mean——?'

'I certainly do,' his sister said. 'Maxim definitely likes to play, as well as work. Although he doesn't usually play on his own doorstep,' she added. 'He's got very definite rules about that. I think that it's to protect William and Alice. He doesn't want them to get attached to any woman he might bring home, because he isn't interested in long-term relationships.' Then she wrinkled her nose. 'I'm talking too much again, I really shouldn't be telling you all this. The trouble is, I absolutely love to gossip. It drives Maxim mad; he hates it when anyone discusses him.'

Cleo was fascinated by these glimpses into Maxim's private life, though. She was itching to ask more questions of his talkative, informative sister, but at that moment the kitchen door reopened and Maxim came back in.

He looked at his sister, and then at the flush that had covered Cleo's face. 'You've been talking about me,' he said at once, his eyes darkening.

His sister looked guilty, but not in the least worried. 'It's entirely your own fault, Maxim. Everyone loves to talk about you, because you never talk about yourself.'

'I don't like it,' he growled at her.

'She really didn't say anything very much,' Cleo said nervously, springing to Sarah's defence.

'She always says too much!' But there was affection, as well as exasperation, in his voice.

Sarah picked up her bag and began to head towards the door. 'Perhaps this is a good time for me to go. Anyway, I've got to cover poor Richard in calamine lotion again, to try and stop him scratching himself to bits. He did cheer up a bit, though, when I told him he wouldn't be able to go back to school next week because he wouldn't be over the chickenpox by then. William and Alice will be all right, of course, they've already had it.' She was just about to whizz out of the door when she stopped again. 'Oh, you have remembered the fund-raising evening at the Templetons' tomorrow, haven't you, Maxim? I'm really counting on your support. Why don't you bring Cleo?' she added, grinning at her brother. 'She'll be good protection against all those predatory matrons with their marriageable daughters!'

She breezed out the door, leaving Cleo feeling faintly exhausted. Even Maxim looked slightly jaded.

He sat down and poured himself some coffee. Then he glanced at Cleo. 'What exactly did my sister tell you about me?'

'Oh—nothing important,' she said hurriedly.

'Mmm,' he said, in clear disbelief.

Cleo decided it was definitely time to change the subject. 'This fund-raising evening tomorrow—what are you raising funds *for*?'

'Remember I told you about the development being planned for this area?'

'The hotel and holiday cottages?'

He nodded. 'Sarah is leading the local protest against it.'

'I should think she'd be very good at something like that.'

'She can certainly talk people into almost anything,' Maxim said wryly. He drank a couple of mouthfuls of coffee, and then pushed the cup away. 'I'm giving her whatever help I can, and introducing her to people who could be useful.'

'Will the protest succeed?'

'I've never known Sarah fail at anything yet.' Then he glanced at his watch. 'It's almost time for William and Alice's tea.'

'Oh, yes, your children,' Cleo said, rather pointedly.

He gave a dry smile. 'All right, I know that I should have mentioned them. But I wasn't expecting them home for a few more days.'

'I saw the toys in the cupboard, and the small-size wellington boots, but I thought you kept them for the children who come here to have their portraits painted. How old are they?' she added.

'William's six and Alice is five.'

'So they were only two and one when their mother died. Hardly old enough to remember her,' she said sadly. She knew what it was like to have no clear memories of your mother, how that emptiness seemed to stay with you for the rest of your life.

Maxim gave a quick frown. 'Sarah talked about my wife?'

'Only because I asked her,' Cleo said hastily. She didn't want to get Sarah into trouble. 'When your children turned up out of the blue, I wondered if a wife was suddenly going to appear, as well. I didn't mean to pry.'

He looked sceptical, but didn't push it any further. 'Your mother died when you were young, didn't she?' he asked unexpectedly.

'Yes, when I was five,' she said in a subdued voice.

'So you know what it's like.'

Cleo nodded. 'How—how did William and Alice's mother die?' she asked in a low voice.

'In a plane crash,' Maxim said, after a short pause. 'It was a small, private plane, and it was being flown by my father. Vivienne worked for him sometimes, organising business conferences. She had a flair for that kind of thing, she loved working with people. They were flying up to Birmingham, to finalise arrangements for a symposium the following month. My father also died in the crash.'

Cleo's eyes shot wide open. 'I didn't know, I'm sorry. I wouldn't have *asked* if I'd known——'

Maxim cut in. 'It's all right. I don't usually talk about it, but—I seem to be able to talk to you. I suppose it's because you've gone through the same kind of thing, losing someone close to you very suddenly.'

'It must have been an awful time for you.'

'Yes, it was. I still miss my father, miss him like hell, although we spent a lot of our adult lives fighting each other because he was a very dominant man, and he didn't like the fact that he couldn't dominate his only son. Vivienne, my wife——' He hesitated for several moments, then went on, 'Our marriage was over a long time before she died. We only stayed together because of William and Alice. It was still a shattering thing to happen, though.'

'You left London and moved up here after your wife died?' Cleo asked a little hesitantly.

'Sarah and her family—she's got three boys and a girl—were already living here. I thought it would be better for William and Alice if we lived nearby. Since they've only got one parent now, they need to keep in touch with the rest of their family. Sarah sometimes has them over for the weekend, and they all go away on holiday together. I'm usually too busy to get away for more than a couple of days at a time.'

'Is it because of the children that you work here, from home?'

Maxim shrugged. 'I used to travel all over the world, accepting commissions. But you can't do that when you're suddenly left responsible for two young children. Luckily, I'd built up my reputation by then, and it turned out that a surprising number of clients were willing to come and stay here while I worked on their portrait.'

'It must have meant quite a change of lifestyle for you,' Cleo said thoughtfully.

'I certainly don't regret or resent the changes I've had to make. And I think that William and Alice are turning out to be two reasonably happy and well adjusted children. That in itself makes the whole thing worthwhile.'

'They certainly look as if they're bursting with health and energy,' Cleo commented drily.

'I think you'll be meeting them again soon. They'll be down again as soon as they've finished putting their things away.' Maxim suddenly grinned. 'Feel up to it?'

'Probably not. I told you, I don't know the first thing about children.'

'Wait until you've got half a dozen of your own. You'll soon learn.'

Cleo immediately stiffened. 'I don't intend to have any children. Not ever,' she said in a tight little voice.

Maxim's own face changed, and his eyes became distinctly cool. 'Because you don't intend to ruin that perfect body of yours by becoming pregnant? Are you so obsessed with the way you look that you can't stand the thought of being rather ungainly for a few months?'

Because I'm terrified by the thought of dying, like my mother! Cleo wanted to shout back at him. Instead, though, her face became pinched and her mouth set into a tight line. 'I'm a model,' she said in a defensive tone. 'I can't afford to ruin my figure.'

'Several top models have taken a year off to have a baby, and then picked up their careers again afterwards with no problems.'

'Well, I'm not going to be one of them,' she retorted. 'Anyway, I'm not even married, so the question doesn't arise.'

'And when it does?' Maxim questioned her, his eyes narrowing.

'It never will, because I'm not *going* to marry.'

'No children, no marriage—it looks as if you're going to have a very self-centred and selfish life,' Maxim said rather harshly. Then his dark eyes locked on to her face, boring right into her. 'But don't act selfishly around my children. Remember that this is their house, their home. Let them know in any way that you dislike them, do one thing to upset them, and you'll be out.'

'I don't dislike them,' Cleo said defensively. 'I just said that I didn't understand them! Look, I'll prove that

I want to be nice to them, I'll—I'll—' She tried hard to think of something she could do. Then her eyes suddenly brightened. 'I'll get their tea for them. They must be hungry, and you're probably too busy to cook for them.'

'But you can't cook,' Maxim reminded her.

'I'm learning!'

'How far have you got in one day?' he asked sceptically.

Cleo tossed back her pale blonde hair. 'I'm sure I can manage tea for two small children! I'm not *totally* stupid or incompetent. What do they like to eat?'

'Anything that's bad for them,' Maxim said drily. 'Like all kids, they love junk food. Chips, beans, sausages, beefburgers—if it's fatty and fried, they'll eat it. The day when I'm going to succeed in convincing them that they like fresh fruit and vegetables and big plates of healthy salads is a long way in the future.'

'Just leave me to get on with it,' Cleo said with some determination, getting to her feet. 'You can go back to work. Do you want me to get tea for you, as well?' she asked as he headed towards the door.

Maxim's eyebrows rose expressively. 'You're volunteering to cook for me?'

'This is a one-off offer,' she said tartly. 'Take it or leave it.'

'Oh, I'll take it.' His eyes gleamed briefly. 'I never like to miss out on a new experience.' Then he left before she had a chance to answer.

Cleo glared briefly at the empty doorway. Then she turned round and began to hunt through the fridge and freezer.

'Chips, baked beans and burgers,' she muttered to herself. 'And I wonder if I could make some kind of cake for afterwards?'

A hunt through the recipe books produced a sponge recipe that looked quick and easy to make. Just mix together the flour, eggs, butter and milk, and spread some jam on after it was cooked. Cleo rummaged through the cupboards, found the ingredients, and quickly began to measure them out.

'This is *easy*,' she said, with growing confidence, running flour-covered fingers through her hair, leaving white streaks behind in their wake.

She whisked the ingredients together—she might not be able to cook, but she was good at using gadgets—spooned the mixture into a tin, and shoved into the oven. Then Cleo began to concentrate on dinner itself.

The freezer produced chips that could be cooked in the oven, she found the hamburgers and put them under the grill, then opened a tin of beans.

'All right, so this is only an easy meal, but I still think too much has been made of this cooking business,' she told herself. 'A child could do this!'

She left the hamburgers to sizzle under the grill as she set the table in the kitchen. She thought this would be a more informal, friendlier place to eat than the dining-room. And she needed all the help she could get, if she was to put right William and Alice's first impressions of her.

The hamburgers were still sizzling, and she could see the beans bubbling. Everything was nearly ready, so she called out that tea was ready, feeling rather proud of herself.

Maxim came in a minute later, with a child on either side of him. Three pairs of dark eyes looked straight at her, completely unnerving Cleo.

'Er—sit down,' she said. 'I've just got to serve it on to the plates.'

As William took his seat, he turned to his father. 'We don't like her,' he said in a loud whisper. 'She shouted at us.'

'William tends to speak his mind,' Maxim said, without a trace of an apology.

'Like father, like son,' Cleo muttered, as she shovelled chips—should they be so pale? she wondered rather anxiously—on to the plates.

'Look, I'm sorry I shouted at you,' she said as she juggled with the hamburgers, which looked *awfully* black, and gave an ominously hard thud as they hit the plates. 'I didn't mean to, but I'd just woken up, and I didn't know who you were or what you were doing in the garden.'

'We were just playing,' said Alice rather primly. 'We live here, we're allowed to do that.'

'Of course you are,' agreed Cleo. She was scraping baked beans out of the saucepan. She hadn't realised that, while the ones on the top had been bubbling away, the ones at the bottom had been sticking to the saucepan like glue! Then she watched their faces apprehensively as she placed their meal in front of them. 'Eat up,' she said encouragingly. 'There's a cake when you've finished this.'

William poked his chips experimentally. 'They're hard,' he said critically. 'You haven't cooked them for long enough.'

'It said twenty minutes on the packet. And I *cooked* them for twenty minutes,' Cleo said defensively.

'At the right number?' Maxim queried gently.

'Well—the cake had to be cooked at one number, and the chips at another, so I picked one in the middle.'

'If you're cooking at a lower number than recommended, you need to leave them in for longer. On the other hand, I think that the hamburgers could have done with a shorter cooking time,' said Maxim with amusement, as he cut into one and sent a charred black lump shooting across his plate.

'The beans aren't too bad,' volunteered Alice.

Cleo felt so grateful for those few kind words that she wanted to swoop down and kiss her.

'This is horrible,' said William gloomily to his father. 'Worse even than school dinner.'

'OK,' said Cleo, scooping up the plates, 'forget the chips and hamburgers, we'll have the cake. It's a sponge. How about that?'

'I like cake,' said Alice happily.

Cleo decided that she definitely liked Alice; this was the kind of child she could get along with. She still had a lot of reservations about William, though.

As soon as she took the sponge cake out of the oven, she knew that it hadn't turned out right. She supposed it was the deep sag in the middle that gave the game away.

Alice peered at it. 'You've put in too much milk,' she announced, with all the authority of an expert. 'It makes it go all soggy.'

Cleo began to have second thoughts about Alice as well. And she was amazed at how upset she felt at the way those three pairs of dark eyes had looked so critically at everything she had put in front of them. Perhaps it wouldn't have been so bad if she hadn't *tried* so hard; she had really wanted to get this right.

'All right, so I can't cook,' she said, trying not to feel totally inadequate. 'I suppose that makes one more thing that I'm no good at. But I don't care, I really *do not care*,' she lied, picking up the soggy sponge cake and dumping it in the bin. 'It isn't important, is it?' she went on, blinking away a sudden tear, 'I mean, the whole world isn't going to collapse just because I can't cook a simple tea?' More tears were coming now, she was horrified to feel them rolling helplessly down her cheeks. 'There are more chips and hamburgers in the freezer, but don't cook any for me, because I'm just not hungry any more,' she said, with a small, tearful hiccup. Then, feeling completely humiliated by her failure, she headed blindly for the door.

As she rushed out, she heard William turn to his father and say, in a rather puzzled voice, 'Why is she crying?'

Cleo didn't hear Maxim's reply. She kept on going, out of the house, into the cool early evening air. She walked across the field, and then sat on a fallen tree-trunk on the far side, staring across at the lake. It was one of the most tranquil scenes she had ever seen, with the sun silently slipping behind the mountains, the sky gently splashed with colour and the shores of the lake slipping into soft darkness as the light began to fade.

She didn't hear Maxim walk up behind her. That was why she jumped so hard when he sat down on the log beside her.

'Go away,' she said in a muffled, slightly shaken voice.

'Still upset because you ruined tea?'

She meant to tell him that she certainly *wasn't* upset. Instead, to her alarm, she found herself blurting out, 'I hate it that I'm so useless at everything!'

'Plenty of people burn hamburgers and cook soggy cakes,' he said equably.

'But I can't do *anything*,' Cleo said miserably.

'You're a top model,' he reminded her. 'That's an achievement.'

'No, it's luck, because I was born with the right face, the right body, the right look. And I only became a model because I didn't know what else to do, I've never known what to do, I'm not really good at anything, just average, and now I'm twenty-three and my life's going nowhere, and I don't know what to do about it!'

Immediately she had confessed all that, she regretted it. Maxim Brenner was *not* the man she should be telling all this to. He couldn't do anything about it, couldn't help in any way. He wouldn't even want to help; she was nothing to him, just someone whose portrait he had to paint, and he hadn't even wanted to do that, he had been pressured into it by her father.

'Forget I said all that,' she muttered. 'I'm just tired, I didn't mean it.'

'I think you meant every word of it,' he said levelly.

'Even if I did, it's not your problem,' Cleo said wearily. 'You've got your own difficulties to cope with. Bringing up two small children and keeping a demanding career going can't be easy.' She got to her feet. 'It's getting chilly, I'm going in.'

She turned around, caught her foot in a clump of grass and stumbled against him. Maxim grabbed hold of her, stopped her from falling, and Cleo caught her breath. She hadn't been prepared for the sudden physical contact, and the strength and hardness of his body caught her unawares.

'I like the feel of your skin,' he said softly, running his fingers down her bare arm.

'What?' she said, in confusion.

'Good texture, soft but firm.'

Cleo remembered that he was an artist, he was probably just being objective.

'I think—you should let go of me,' she said rather jerkily.

'I'm not holding you.'

She was alarmed to discover that he was right, she was still leaning against him, but she was perfectly free to move away—if she wanted to.

And, of course, she *did* want to, she told herself nervously.

Maxim's fingers moved down to her wrist. 'Nice bones,' he murmured.

She gave an edgy laugh that didn't sound quite right. 'You're making me sound like an anatomy lesson.'

'I'm simply appreciating some of your good qualities. You seem to think that you don't have any at all, but you're wrong about that, Cleo.'

She hadn't heard quite that note in his voice before. She became aware of the gathering dusk around her, the seductive stillness of the evening.

'You also have a very nice mouth,' Maxim went on, his voice a tone lower now and as velvet smooth as the touch of his fingers against her skin. 'I'm going to enjoy painting it.' He raised one hand and lightly traced the outline of it with just one finger. Cleo could feel her lips actually quivering, and clamped her mouth shut to try and stop the betraying tremor.

He's going to kiss me, she thought a little wildly. And I'm going to freeze up, the way I always do. Then he'll know what else is wrong with me!

Maxim looked at her thoughtfully. Then, almost experimentally, he bent his head and let his mouth drift gently against hers.

Cleo felt her muscles tense, and her mouth clamped shut, instinctively shutting him out.

Maxim immediately drew back again. His dark eyes locked on to hers, and this time there was a new and questioning intensity in his gaze.

'Problems, Cleo?' he said softly.

'Why do men always think you've got a problem, just because you don't want to kiss them?' she challenged him with edgy defiance.

'All you've got to do is say no.' There was an edge to his own tone, now.

'Then I'm saying it,' she retorted. 'No!'

'And are you just saying no to me? Or do you say it to everyone?'

His perceptiveness deeply alarmed her. 'That's none of your business,' she got out.

'While you're staying in my house, everything about you is my business.' His dark eyes fixed on her. 'Tell me about it, Cleo.'

And oh, God, she wanted to! That was the most frightening thing of all.

With an enormous effort, she dragged her own hugely dilated eyes away from his face.

'There's nothing to talk about,' she said tightly. 'And if you've got to have an explanation, then just tell yourself that it's one more thing that I'm no good at!'

Then she broke away from him before he could ask more questions, and raced back to the house.

CHAPTER FIVE

CLEO went straight to her own rooms in the annexe. She slammed the door behind her, and then went through to the small sitting-room, where she slumped down into the chair. Today had been a total disaster! Trying to turn Maxim's children out of their own home, ruining dinner, and then messing up that kiss. And it probably would have been a very nice kiss, if only she had been able to relax and enjoy it. She was quite sure that Maxim was *very* good at that kind of thing.

She gave a deep sigh. That was just one more area of her life she needed to change. Only it was hard to see how she was ever going to manage it. How could she possibly enjoy making love, when she was so scared to death of getting pregnant all the time? One simply cancelled out the other; there couldn't be any real pleasure when the dominant emotion was always fear.

For a long time, Cleo sat in the chair and stared rather despairingly at the wall. No one knew about her secret fears—she couldn't seem to talk about them to anyone, they just stayed locked up inside her. Once or twice she had wondered if she should try and get some expert help, but in the end she had always shied away from it. This was something that she needed to work out for herself, she had told herself—only she didn't have the slightest idea how to do it.

Nearly half an hour later there was a light knock on the door. Cleo's heart gave a sudden thump, and she had to force herself to get up and open it.

Maxim stood on the other side, his face and dark eyes giving away absolutely nothing as he studied her own rather drawn features. Cleo stared back at him with a touch of defiance.

'Look, I don't want to talk about what happened,' she told him.

'I haven't come here to discuss anything,' he replied. 'Only to tell you that supper's ready.'

Cleo gazed at him rather blankly. 'Supper?' she echoed at last.

'You haven't eaten anything since lunchtime. I don't want to send you back to your father looking like a skeleton, or he'll accuse me of mistreating you.'

'I'm—I'm not hungry,' she muttered.

'Of course you are. Come and eat, before the steaks get cold,' he ordered calmly.

Cleo found herself following him to the kitchen, even though she hadn't had any intention of going. She didn't think she liked that. How had this man made her do something that she hadn't wanted to do?

She decided not to think about it right now, because the whole thing was slightly alarming. Instead, she sat down at the table and then looked at her plate, which held fresh salad and a perfectly grilled steak.

'Did you cook this?'

'It wasn't the hardest thing I've ever done,' Maxim said, his eyes glinting with amusement.

'I suppose that you cooked tea for William and Alice, as well?' she mumbled, remembering that her attempt had been dumped in the bin.

'Don't look so downcast. Hardly anyone gets things right the first time.'

'I bet you do,' Cleo said at once. 'You're probably the sort of man who's good at absolutely everything!'

Maxim gave a rather wicked grin. 'There are quite a few things that I've been told I'm very good at.' Then he went on in a slightly more serious tone, 'But as far as William and Alice are concerned, I made dozens of mistakes when I was first left on my own with them. You learn from experience, though, and you gradually begin to get it right.'

'Was your wife a good mother?' Cleo asked, without really thinking. Then she looked at him anxiously because that had been a personal question, and she had already learnt that he didn't like those.

Maxim answered after only a moment's hesitation, though. 'Yes, she was. I think that surprised her, as much as anyone else, because she was the very last person you would have expected to be the maternal type. When you have a child, though, a whole new range of emotions suddenly seem to get kickstarted into life. I don't think Vivienne was prepared for that. She let herself get pregnant because she knew that our marriage wasn't working, and it was the one thing that would stop me walking out. She enjoyed it so much, though, that she became pregnant again with Alice as soon as she could after giving birth to William.'

Cleo felt a small, cold shiver run through her. She simply couldn't imagine anyone wanting to go through the ordeal of pregnancy twice, in such a short time.

'Didn't you hate her for doing that?' she said in a low voice. 'After all, the children tied you to a marriage that you wanted to get away from.'

'I've never regretted the birth of William and Alice,' Maxim said sharply. 'They may have cost me my freedom, but that was a price I was more than willing to pay.'

'Where your children are concerned, you're certainly very defensive!'

'Of course I am. If you had children of your own, you'd understand why. But you don't intend to let a child spoil your perfect body or disrupt your easy, pleasant lifestyle, do you?' he said levelly.

'I'm entitled to make that decision, aren't I?' she said defiantly.

'Of course. But have you ever stopped to think what you'll be missing out on? Children can be infuriating, time-consuming and exhausting, but they bring dozens of new, small pleasures to make up for all of that. And it's fascinating to watch them grow and develop. They're small dynamos of energy and enthusiasm, hungry all the time for knowledge and new experiences.'

But Cleo had closed her mind to what he was saying. She had become very good at doing that, when the subject of children came up. If a friend became pregnant she would shut them out, both physically and mentally. She would find excuses not to see them, would stop even thinking about them. And if they insisted on coming round to show off the new baby when it finally arrived, she would force herself to make a couple of polite remarks and then find some excuse to leave the room.

'I'm simply not interested in children or marriage,' she said in a rather stiff voice. Then she pushed her plate away. 'Thank you for supper. I'm going to bed now.'

Maxim's dark gaze fixed on her. 'Like me to come with you?'

At first, she thought that she had misheard him. Then she realised that she hadn't. 'No, I would not!' she said with fast growing fierceness. 'How dare you say something like that?'

Maxim gave an unconcerned shrug. 'You don't intend to marry and I'm certainly not looking for a wife. We seem like an ideally matched pair.'

'We are not matched in any way,' Cleo retorted, still outraged. 'I didn't even like it when you kissed me!'

'You didn't let yourself like it,' Maxim corrected her. 'And why all this over-reaction, Cleo? You must have had offers like this before.'

'Yes, but I didn't expect one from *you*.'

His eyes gleamed darkly. 'Why not?'

'Because—well, for one thing, your sister said that you never played around on your own doorstep.'

'Rules are made to be broken occasionally,' he told her in a velvet voice. Then he looked at her more intently. 'Wouldn't you like to break some rules with me, Cleo?'

'N-no,' she stuttered, finding it much harder than she had expected to get out that one word. And she knew that if she didn't drag her eyes away from that dark, powerful gaze of his very soon, then she was *never* going to be able to look away. And what would happen then?

Cleo scrambled to her feet, almost knocking over her chair. 'I'm—I'm going back to my room,' she got out in a strangled voice.

'Don't worry,' Maxim said in a more relaxed tone, 'I'm not going to try and stop you.'

'I'm not worried,' she retorted. 'Not about one single little thing!'

'No, of course you're not,' he agreed, and his eyes had begun to glitter with amusement. 'Goodnight, Cleo. Sleep well.'

And the lightly mocking tone of his voice made it very clear that he knew she wasn't going to sleep well at all.

Cleo escaped from the kitchen as quickly as she could. Once she was back in the annexe she got some control over her breathing and calmed down a little. All right, so he had virtually told her that he would like to go to bed with her. Other men had told her the same thing—with her looks and body, it would be surprising if they hadn't—but it had never been a problem before.

And was it a problem this time? she asked herself uneasily.

She soon convinced herself that it wasn't. She had given him the usual firm refusal, and he had seemed to accept it. No, it had been an awkward—and unexpected!—moment, but she had dealt with it, it was over now, and it wasn't likely to occur again.

Cleo gave a small sigh. How she wished she could avoid this kind of situation completely. It just wasn't possible, though. Men found her physically attractive, and short of turning herself into a total frump there wasn't anything she could do about it. In fact, several of the invitations she had received in the past had been a lot more serious than Maxim's, with a ring being unexpectedly produced on one memorable occasion. Cleo had invented a dozen different and inventive excuses for turning them down, though. And, whenever she could, she tried to make sure that it simply didn't happen. When she went out, she usually tried to make sure that it was with a group of friends. And on the rare occasions that she did go out on a single date, she always suggested going to a place where there would be plenty of other people around. And as soon as her date started to want something more than a few goodnight kisses, she dropped them.

When she finally went to bed, she didn't sleep at all well. In the morning, though, the sun was still shining, the fields, lake and mountains basked tranquilly in the soft golden light, and Cleo felt much more relaxed as she pulled on dark leggings and a bright purple T-shirt. She didn't bother with make up; she left her pale blonde hair soft and loose instead of curling it, and pulled on a favourite pair of old trainers.

She certainly hadn't forgotten everything that had happened last night, but she was determined not to make a big thing of it. There had been a kiss, Maxim had made a pass at her, and she had turned it down. No big deal. In fact, it was probably something that had been bound to happen at some time or other, under the circumstances. Almost a ritual that they had had to go through. It was behind them, now, and they could forget about it.

Cleo bounced into the kitchen, hungry and ready for breakfast. It definitely took the edge off her appetite, though, when she saw all three Brenners sitting at the table, and three pairs of dark eyes swivelled round to fix on her as she came through the door.

'I—er—I thought I was the only one up,' she said, staring warily back at them.

'Do you think we lie in bed all morning?' asked Maxim with amusement.

'I wish that I *could* stay in bed all day,' said William at once. 'Then I wouldn't have to go to school.'

'Don't you like school?' asked Cleo, sitting down next to him and reaching for the cereal.

He shrugged. 'I suppose it's OK. I'd rather play football, though. Or have a go on my computer.' Then he looked critically at Cleo as she sprinkled a very generous spoonful of sugar over her cereal. 'That isn't good for you. It makes holes in your teeth, and you have to have fillings when you go to the dentist.'

'It looks as if some of the lectures I keep giving him are finally starting to get through,' Maxim said drily.

'What should I put on my cereal?' Cleo asked William.

'Raisins or banana or apple. And in the summer, we sometimes have strawberries.'

'Well, all of those things sound a lot nicer than sugar. I'll have banana tomorrow morning, and apple the day after.'

'And what will you have the day after that?' asked Alice, who had been following the conversation with some interest.

'Raisins,' said Cleo.

'And the day after that? You can't have strawberries,' Alice told her. 'They're all gone now, we can't have them again until next year.'

'She could have burnt hamburgers,' said William, and both children collapsed into loud giggles.

'That's enough,' Maxim said with mock sternness. 'Why don't the two of you go out and play, if you've finished your breakfast? You'd better make the most of the next few days; you'll be back at school next week.'

Both of them gave loud, exaggerated groans, and then headed out the door. Left alone with Maxim, Cleo immediately felt a lot less relaxed. To try and cover up her sudden nervousness, she began to chatter.

'William and Alice seem to have forgotten about the bad start we got off to yesterday.'

'Children don't bear grudges,' Maxim said. 'Only adults do that.' He glanced at his watch. 'I've a couple of free hours this morning. When you've finished breakfast, I want you to come along to the studio. If I don't make a start on your portrait soon, you'll be here all winter.'

'I'll have to curl my hair and do something to my face. And I need to change my clothes——'

'I don't want you to do anything to any part of you,' he cut in with a touch of impatience. 'Come along just the way you are right now.'

'In an old T-shirt and leggings?' Cleo said in disbelief. 'But you can't paint me like this!'

'Why not? You look more relaxed and natural than at any time since you arrived here.'

'But that isn't the kind of portrait my father wants,' she argued.

'How do you know that? Perhaps he'd like to see you looking like yourself for once, instead of always looking as if you're about to be photographed for some magazine cover.'

'But he wants a *formal* portrait,' she insisted.

'When we made the initial arrangements, your father didn't specify any particular kind of portrait at all.'

Cleo thought of the painting of her mother, that her own portrait was to hang alongside.

'You don't understand——' she began. Then she stopped, because she didn't want to get involved in a lot of very personal explanations.

'What don't I understand?' Maxim said at once, his eyes narrowing. 'What's the big secret, Cleo?'

'No secret,' she muttered. 'I just know what my father likes, that's all.'

He looked at her steadily for a very long time, his dark gaze fixed on her in a way that made her nerves jangle disconcertingly. Just when Cleo was thinking that she couldn't take that intense scrutiny for one second longer, the door burst open and William came in, closely followed by Alice.

'There's a red sports car outside,' William announced.

'Yes, it's mine,' said Cleo. 'Didn't you see it yesterday, when your aunt brought you home?'

William shook his head. 'It really is yours?' he said, clearly impressed.

'It really is,' Cleo told him gravely.

It was obvious from the look on his face that she had just shot up in his estimation.

'Can you take us to school in it next week?' he said with enthusiasm. Then he turned to Maxim. 'Imagine what Dean and Robert will say if I turn up in that. Their eyes will pop right out!'

'I hope not,' said Maxim drily. 'And I don't even know if Cleo will still be here by next week. As soon as I've finished her portrait, she's going home.'

'Then paint it very, *very* slowly,' William instructed his father. Then he rushed out of the kitchen again, closely followed by Alice.

'Unless you get yourself along to the studio, I'm not going to get any painting done at all,' Maxim said pointedly.

Cleo finished the last of her cereal and gulped down some coffee. 'I'm ready,' she announced. Then she wrinkled her nose. 'I still think I should change my clothes.'

The look on Maxim's face told her that *wasn't* a good idea, and she gave a small grimace, then hurried along to the studio.

Maxim worked on her portrait for the rest of the morning. After trying several poses, he finally had her sit in a chair by the window in a very relaxed position, looking out towards the lake. He covered the canvas with a thin wash of burnt umber, then quickly and expertly painted in the rough outline of her head and body. Then he began to draw in more detail, his dark gaze skimming over her, studying her with an intensity that made Cleo feel slightly breathless.

'Can I talk?' she asked at last, finding it harder and harder just to sit there, pinned down by those dark eyes.

'As long as you don't move.'

'I won't,' she promised. 'I'd like to know more about the way you work, though. For a start, why do I have to stay in your house all this time? A lot of portrait painters work from photographs, don't they? Why couldn't I sit for you a couple of times, and then let you finish the portrait using photos?'

'I'm not interested in the way other painters work,' Maxim replied. 'And I never use photographs, I only paint live subjects.' His eyes briefly fixed on her face. 'Are you tired of staying here? Do you want to run back home? To Daddy?'

'No, I don't,' Cleo said with a grimace. 'For one thing, I don't want to tell him that you're painting me wearing a purple T-shirt and leggings! This wasn't at *all* the kind of portrait he had in mind when he commissioned you. You do realise that he'll probably ask for his money back, when he finally sees it?'

'That'll be difficult, because he isn't paying me for the portrait,' Maxim said. Then he added, 'Kick off those trainers. You've got nice feet, I think I'll paint you barefooted.'

Cleo had just begun to unlace her trainers when she realised what he had said. With a frown, she looked at him. 'What do you mean, he isn't paying you for the portrait? When I first came here, you told me he'd paid in advance.'

'He did give me a substantial sum of money,' Maxim agreed. 'But not for the portrait. It was a donation to the Brenner Trust. He only gave the money, though, on the condition that I painted your portrait.'

'In other words, he bribed you!' she said indignantly.

Maxim shrugged. 'Yes, I suppose he did. He knew that it was the one way he could get me to accept the commission. I often turn down clients, but I never refuse substantial donations to the Trust, no matter what strings are attached.'

'What *is* the Brenner Trust?' she asked with a small frown.

'It was set up by my father, and it uses part of the large amount of wealth he accumulated during his lifetime, plus any additional donations, to educate children in underdeveloped countries. Money from the trust can be used to pay for anything from a basic primary education to a university degree course. Since my father made a lot of his money overseas, this was his way of putting something back, something that will hopefully help to build a better and more equal future for those countries.'

'Who runs the Trust?'

'It's run by professional managers, but I have overall control,' Maxim told her. 'It's time-consuming, because I take a very active interest, but the more efficiently the Trust is administered, the more money there is available for the actual educational grants.'

She shook her head. 'You're full of surprises. I learn something new about you every day!'

He gave a sudden, wicked grin. 'That should make the next few days very interesting. Incidentally, are you coming with me to the Templetons' tonight?'

'Who are the Templetons?' Cleo demanded, her nerves beginning to feel very brittle. Then her brows drew lightly together. 'Oh, wait a minute, I remember. They're holding some kind of fund-raising party to help your sister fight the proposed development.'

'The Templetons have lived around here for generations,' Maxim told her. 'Old family, lots of money, a huge house and a great deal of influence. I've persuaded them to back Sarah in her campaign against the development. Tonight, anyone who comes up with a sizeable donation can wander around the Templetons' house, take a close look at their antiques, nibble dainty little sandwiches and rub shoulders with some of the most prestigious families in the county.'

'Like the Brenners?' Cleo said drily.

'Do you think we're a prestigious family?' Maxim asked with amusement.

'I'm sure you are. Especially since your father was knighted for services to industry. I mean, he *was* Sir Hugh Brenner, wasn't he?'

Maxim's face changed considerably. 'Yes, he was,' he said after a short pause. 'How did you know that? I didn't tell you.'

'When you told me about the plane crash, I suddenly put two and two together. I remembered reading about it in the papers, there was a lot of news coverage at the time. And I realised that I'd heard my father talk about him a couple of times in the past. Sir Hugh Brenner was famous. And your mother——' Cleo suddenly stopped dead, because she realised that she hadn't once heard Maxim mention his mother. Why? she wondered. He had talked about the rest of his family. Perhaps this was a subject she shouldn't have raised...

From the look on Maxim's face, she knew that she had guessed right. His mouth had set into a slightly bitter line, and his eyes had darkened. 'Oh, yes, my mother,' he said at last, in a very different tone of voice. 'My mother is famous as well, isn't she? Socially prominent—I believe that's the way they generally describe her. List the events that are considered the social highlights of the year and she'll be at every one of them. Throw a ball or a garden party and you can guarantee my mother will be there. When we were children, I don't remember her being at home for a single evening. She's been in America for the last year, because she considered that the American social scene was an Everest that she hadn't yet climbed. And, of course, she's managed it. She's on the "A" list for every party, she's shaken every famous hand, been photographed with everyone worth being seen with. With the combination of a title and a pedigree that stretches back hundreds of years, my mother is unstoppable.'

Cleo didn't know what to say. All that pent-up bitterness—she certainly hadn't expected *that*. She fervently wished she had never mentioned his mother! If he had had a neglected childhood, though, with his father wrapped up in his business affairs and his mother flitting from one social event to another, it certainly explained why Maxim was so determined that his own children should have a stable, happy home life with a parent who was always there.

'I—er—I'd like to come to the Templetons' tonight,' she said at last, trying to steer the conversation back to a safer subject. 'I want to help your sister with the fund raising.'

'Why?' Maxim said bluntly. 'It isn't your fight; it isn't anything to do with you.'

Cleo bristled slightly. 'It's the kind of fight that everyone should be involved in. Yes, holiday cottages are very nice, but it's far more important that affordable homes should be built for young people. Or do you think I'm too dumb to realise that?'

'No, I don't think you're dumb,' he said, after a short pause. 'And if you want to come tonight, Sarah would be pleased to see you there.'

But will *you* be pleased? Cleo wanted to ask him. She didn't say it out loud, though.

Maxim threw a cloth over the canvas, and it was clear that no more work would be done on her portrait today. Cleo left the studio, nibbled half-heartedly at a couple of sandwiches for lunch, then sat in the garden for an hour, trying to concentrate on a book.

Later in the afternoon, she began to get herself ready for the Templetons' party tonight. William and Alice wandered into the annexe halfway through. William soon got bored, watching her curl her hair, but Alice was fascinated.

'Can you curl *my* hair?' she asked a little shyly.

'Of course,' Cleo said promptly, and she spent the next quarter of an hour expertly twisting Alice's long, dark hair around the hot brush, coaxing it into a mass of ringlets.

'The curls won't last,' Cleo warned. 'They're just for a special occasion, like a party—or going out with a new boyfriend,' she added, with a grin.

Alice pulled a face. 'I don't want a boyfriend. Boys are silly, they run around a lot and shout and show off.' Then she looked more thoughtful. 'You're going out with my daddy tonight, aren't you? Is he your boyfriend?'

'No, he certainly is *not*,' Cleo said at once. 'I mean, we are going out tonight, but we're just friends. Well, not even friends, really. We're just going to this party together.'

'I saw him kiss you last night,' Alice said matter-of-factly.

Cleo nearly fell off her seat with shock. 'How—how did you manage to see that, Alice?' she managed to splutter at last.

'I was looking out of the window,' Alice went on in the same unconcerned voice. 'I saw you standing in the field with my daddy, and you were talking, and then he kissed you. Then you ran away. Didn't you like the way he kissed you?' she asked with interest.

Cleo swallowed very hard. 'It had—had nothing to do with liking or not liking the way your daddy kissed me,' she finally got out in a slightly strangled tone. 'I'm sure your daddy is very good at kissing. But I told you, he isn't my boyfriend. Anyway, you shouldn't let anyone kiss you unless you know them really well.'

'Why not?'

Cleo knew that she was getting further and further out of her depth.

'That's something you should ask your father,' she said firmly, deciding that she had to put a stop to this conversation. 'He'll explain it to you.'

'I'll go and ask him right now,' Alice said, and she turned round and headed for the door.

'No, I don't think that's a good idea,' Cleo called after her in alarm, but it was already too late, Alice had gone.

With a small groan, Cleo turned back to the mirror. This definitely *wasn't* a good start to the evening! She could hardly back out now, though.

She shrugged off her bathrobe and wriggled into her dress, a sophisticated little number that had been a real showstopper when she had worn it at a recent fashion show. Sleeveless and strapless, it was a startling pink and fitted like a glove over her breasts, waist and hips before flaring out into a short skirt that definitely did great things for her legs.

Cleo ran her fingers through her pale blonde curls so that they cascaded down to her shoulders in a soft tangle, slid her feet into high-heeled sandals that added to her already impressive height, and then headed downstairs.

Maxim was already waiting for her in the entrance hall, and her eyes opened very wide when she saw him. In casual clothes, he looked pretty impressive. But dressed in a dark evening suit, with a crisp white shirt to show off his tan and the discreet glint of gold cuff-links at his wrists, he was an absolute knockout!

He looked up at her as she came down the stairs, and his own eyes registered appreciation.

'We make an interesting couple,' he commented. 'I should think a few eyebrows are going to fly upwards when we're seen together tonight.'

'Just as long as everyone realises that we're also a very *temporary* couple,' Cleo retorted at once. 'I don't want anyone getting the wrong idea!'

'How could they possibly do that?' Maxim asked lightly, as he shepherded her towards the door. 'Incidentally,' he went on, 'Alice has been asking some very interesting questions about kissing. What kind of answers do you think I ought to give her?'

'I've no idea,' she said edgily. 'That's your problem, not mine.'

'I think that it is your problem. You see, she saw you running away after you were kissed. That's made her think that kissing might be something that's not very nice, and I don't want her to grow up with that impression. So—what are you going to do about it, Cleo?'

'Nothing at all!'

'Oh, I think you are,' Maxim warned softly. 'But before you can convince anyone else that kissing can be very nice indeed, you have to believe it yourself. And you don't, do you? Not yet.'

'What do you mean, not yet?' she asked warily as he opened the door for her.

But Maxim merely smiled—a very *wolfish* smile—and didn't answer as he followed her out into the gathering dusk.

CHAPTER SIX

MAXIM'S car was standing outside, large, dark and expensive. 'Not as much fun as a small red sports car,' he commented as he slid into the driving seat beside her, 'but more practical when you've got two small children.'

'The children,' Cleo suddenly repeated, with a worried frown. 'We can't leave them on their own while we go off to a party!'

One of Maxim's dark eyebrows gently rose. 'Do you think I'd do something like that? Mrs Branson is baby-sitting for the evening. She's in the kitchen with them right now, making home-made fudge that will probably make William feel very sick later on because he always bolts down too much of it.'

Cleo relaxed again a little, and the car moved off smoothly and quietly, with Maxim guiding it expertly along the narrow road.

'How far is it to the Templetons'?' she asked a few moments later.

'Not far at all. Their house is half a mile on the other side of the village.'

Lights were just beginning to come on in the village as they passed through, giving the cottages a warm, homely glow. And the lake and the mountains were fading into muted shades of grey, blue and mauve, with a faint sprinkling of stars appearing overhead.

After the village had been left behind, the road began to climb. Soon afterwards, they turned off on to a wide gravel driveway that led up to a large house set high on the hillside, with a superb view over the lake below. A couple of dozen cars were already lined up outside, lights blazed out from every window in the house, and the front doors stood wide open.

'We don't have to stay too long,' said Maxim, bringing the car to a halt. 'We'll say hello to a few people, sample some of the food, drop a donation in the collecting box by the door, and then leave.'

'Don't you like parties?' Cleo said in surprise.

He shrugged. 'I can live without them. The Templetons are pleasant people, though, and they've certainly worked hard to support Sarah's campaign. The least we can do is support their fund-raising effort.'

She followed Maxim into the house, which seemed to be filled with people. Cleo could see at once that most of them seemed to be dripping with very visible assets. There was a lot of gold jewellery set with glittering stones, wafer-thin watches on well-tanned wrists, designer dresses and hand-tailored suits. When it came to fund-raising, the Templetons, with their large stock of very well-heeled friends, were obviously valuable people to have on your side! She wondered how many of them had been personally persuaded by Maxim to support his sister's campaign. She was quite sure that he had a great deal of influence, and that he wouldn't hesitate to use it to get something that he wanted.

Cleo was glad that she had gone to some trouble over her own appearance. Her dress was by one of the top young designers, and as she and Maxim slowly circulated around the room, she knew that they were attracting more than their fair share of attention. Several overdressed mothers with obviously unattached daughters in tow shot dark glances in her direction, and she remembered Maxim's sister mischievously commenting that taking Cleo to the party would protect Maxim from the matrons with their unmarried daughters. Cleo began to realise just how eligible Maxim was, and what a catch he would be for one of these girls. An international reputation as a painter, those rather ravishing looks, a tragic past—what woman could resist him?

She could! Cleo told herself staunchly. All the same, she had to admit that she was rather enjoying all the envious glances that were being covertly thrown her way.

'Do you want something to drink?' Maxim asked.

'Yes, please,' she said at once. It was always a little nerve-racking to walk into a party where you didn't know anyone.

Maxim brought her a glass of champagne—very *good* champagne, Cleo discovered, as she sipped it. Then she looked around the room. Most of the people here seemed to know Maxim; they had greeted him by name and were obviously pleased to see him. During the four years he had lived here, he had certainly integrated himself well into the community. But she supposed he had done it on purpose, because he would be providing roots for his children, as well as himself.

She was just about to ask him whether he planned to live here for the rest of his life when a girl pushed her way purposefully through the throng of well-dressed people towards them. She was small, dark haired and very pretty. As she drew nearer, she shot a look of cool dislike at Cleo, and at the same time laid her hand on Maxim's arm in a proprietorial way.

'Maxim, I thought you weren't coming,' she said, smiling up at him.

'I promised Sarah that I would,' he said, with an answering smile. 'And I always keep my promises.'

'And you've brought a friend?' said the girl, with a subtle emphasis on the word 'friend'.

'This is Cleo Rossiter,' Maxim said. 'She's staying with me at the moment; I'm painting her portrait. Cleo, this is Jane, she's the Templetons' daughter.'

The Templetons' unmarried daughter? Cleo was tempted to ask with a small grin. Just in time, she stopped herself. Poor Maxim—no wonder he hated coming to parties. Every unattached woman in the room was stalking him!

'Will you dance with me?' Jane was now asking, still smiling prettily up at Maxim.

'If Cleo doesn't mind,' Maxim said, at the same time shooting an expressive look in Cleo's direction.

'No, I don't mind at all,' said Cleo cheerfully, totally ignoring the silent signals Maxim was sending her.

He turned round and glowered at her as Jane hauled him off, and Cleo grinned back. If Maxim was irresistible to women, that was his problem, not hers!

'Hello,' said a familiar voice from just behind her. 'I'm glad you've come tonight. Have you been here long?'

It was Sarah, Maxim's sister. She was clutching an empty champagne glass and looking round for one that was full.

'Here,' said Cleo, grabbing one off a passing tray and handing it to her.

'Thanks,' said Sarah. She took a long drink and then sighed happily. 'Mmm, I love this stuff, I could drink gallons of it. I sent my husband off ten minutes ago to get me some more, but he hasn't come back yet. When he finally turns up, I'll introduce you. Where's Maxim? Has he deserted you?'

Cleo pointed to the far end of the room, where the floor had been cleared for dancing. Jane had wound herself possessively around Maxim, and was now slinkily rubbing herself against him in time to the soft beat of the music, practically seducing him right there in the centre of the dance floor.

Sarah gave a faint groan. 'Jane Templeton's been chasing after Maxim from the moment she first set eyes on him. Maxim isn't interested, of course, but she just doesn't seem to be getting the message.'

'Are you sure he isn't interested?' Cleo said doubtfully. 'She's very pretty.'

'She's also got pots of money, and she's probably terrific in bed. But look at Maxim. Even from this distance, you can see he's bored.'

Cleo found it hard to believe that any man could be bored with someone like Jane Templeton wrapped round them so very tightly.

'Jane isn't his type?' she ventured.

'She tries too hard,' Sarah said, with a small shake of her head. 'Most men like to do the chasing; they don't like to *be* chased. Jane keeps trying to seduce him, but that's a real turn-off for someone like Maxim. If there's any seducing to be done, then he's the one who'll do it.'

'And I'm sure he's very good at it,' Cleo said drily.

'He certainly is,' Sarah agreed, with a grin. 'Before he was married, I always used to be very wary about introducing him to any of my girlfriends. They only had to spend an hour alone with him, and they'd go totally moony-eyed and be ready to jump straight into bed with him. It was quite a relief when he married Vivienne and took himself out of circulation.'

'Do you mind if I ask you something?' Cleo said rather hesitantly.

'Of course not,' Sarah said promptly. 'I'll talk about absolutely anything. In fact, Maxim always says that it's a job to *stop* me talking.'

'Well—what did Maxim's wife look like?'

'Vivienne? She was small, very beautiful, very sexy, lots of chestnut-brown hair, and the most gorgeous blue eyes. After their marriage, though, Maxim gradually became disillusioned with her. Vivienne became careless, she let him see that she had been attracted by his money and his growing reputation as much as she had been by him. When Maxim was almost at the point of walking out, though, Vivienne became pregnant. She obviously did it on purpose, to stop Maxim going. She wasn't the type to let a rich husband walk out on her. And yet she turned out to be a surprisingly good mother; she really loved those kids.' Then Sarah gave a small grimace. 'I probably shouldn't be telling you all this. You know how angry Maxim gets when anyone talks about him behind his back.'

'I won't tell him,' Cleo assured her. Then she wrinkled his nose. 'He hasn't had a lot of luck with the women in his life, has he? He chose the wrong wife, and from what he's told me he didn't get very much love and attention from his mother, either.' Then her green eyes flew wide open. 'Oops, sorry,' she said, very apologetically. 'I forgot, she's your mother, too.'

'That's all right,' Sarah said with resignation. 'Maxim and I long ago got used to the fact that we were going to have to grow up without much help from either parent.' Then she began to look at Cleo with new interest. 'I'm amazed that Maxim even mentioned the subject of our mother, though. Usually, he never talks to anyone about his personal life.'

'Oh—really?' Cleo said with sudden caution. Sarah's eyes were beginning to glint with the light of the born matchmaker. 'I'm sure he was simply making polite conversation,' she went on hurriedly.

'Maxim never makes polite conversation,' Sarah said, still looking at Cleo speculatively.

She was saved from having to make any reply because Maxim returned at that point.

His gaze fixed on Cleo rather sternly. 'I brought you with me so that I wouldn't have to spend the evening trying to escape from women like Jane Templeton.'

'It isn't my fault if they take one look at you and hear wedding bells,' Cleo pointed out.

'Don't *you* hear them?' Sarah asked slyly.

'Cleo doesn't intend to get married,' Maxim answered for her. 'That's why she makes the perfect houseguest and the ideal person to bring to a party.'

'Why don't you want to get married?' Sarah asked at once.

Maxim gave a resigned sigh. 'Sarah, don't you ever stop asking questions?'

'No,' she said cheerfully.

'Then I'll have to take Cleo away before she throws something at you, to try and shut you up. Come and dance with me,' he instructed Cleo, 'before I'm carried off by another designing woman.'

With his fingers clasped around her wrist, pulling her firmly in the direction of the dance floor, Cleo didn't get much chance to protest. The music had changed to a slow, smoochy beat and as Maxim held her close—far *too* close, in her opinion—she could see Jane Templeton glowering at them in the background.

'I don't think Jane approves of this,' Cleo said wryly.

'That's the whole idea,' Maxim told her. 'Jane's a nice girl, but I'm not interested in her and I certainly don't want to marry her. The sooner she gets that message, the better.'

'Women don't usually give up that easily,' she warned.

'I've already found that out,' he said with some resignation. 'The more I back off, the more determined they seem to chase after me.'

'Er—talking of backing off,' Cleo said a little uncomfortably, 'do we really need to dance this closely?'

'No, we don't need to,' Maxim agreed equably. 'But I want to.'

She looked up at him warily. 'Why?'

'Because I'm enjoying it. And there won't be any problems or complications with you, will there, Cleo? You're not interested in marriage, you're not going to try and seduce me, turn up on my doorstep at inconvenient times, or fawn and gush over my kids in an effort to impress me.'

'They really do that?' she said, slightly shocked. 'Use your children to try and get your attention?'

'You'd be surprised how many of them turn up with "a small present for William and Alice".' His face briefly darkened. 'That makes me really angry. Children should never be used for any purpose in any relationship.' Then he relaxed again. 'But I'm fairly sure I can trust you, since all you've ever given my kids is burnt hamburgers,' he said with a grin.

'Aren't you *ever* going to let me forget that?' she said with a touch of annoyance.'

'Probably not. It's the most entertaining meal we've had in our house for a long time.' Then the grin disappeared from Maxim's face again, and he gave a faint growl. 'Jane has just been joined by Marion Castleton.

The two of them seem to think they're in some sort of competition to see who can win me.'

'Most men would be flattered by all this female attention,' Cleo pointed out.

'I just find it tiresome. Move a little nearer and try to look as if you find me irresistable,' he instructed. Then his dark eyebrows gently rose. 'Or is that too hard for you?'

But, rather alarmingly, Cleo wasn't finding it hard at all. His hands, as they rested against her, were relaxed and undemanding, and his body was hard and warm. And she could feel a small glow inside her, as if something were responding to that warmth. Don't let down your guard, she warned herself silently. There's something very deceptive about this man, he's too much in control, he's holding too much back. There's a lot of bitterness, anger—passion—locked up inside of him. And if he ever lets go, sets it free...

She gave a small, involuntary shiver. Maxim immediately felt it, and frowned down at her.

'What is it?'

'Nothing,' she muttered.

'You don't like being this close to me?'

'I—it isn't that—I don't want——'

'There's something wrong with you, isn't there?' he cut in, his eyes narrowing. 'Something that you won't talk about, something that you don't want anyone to know about.'

'Of course not——' Cleo began to say, but then stopped because he had caught hold of her wrist and was leading her away from the dance floor, out through the open french windows, into the cool, dark night outside.

'What are you doing?' she said jerkily.

'Taking you somewhere where we can talk.'

'I don't *want* to talk,' she said at once, in a stubborn tone.

'No, I'm quite sure you don't. But I've told you things about myself that are personal, private. I think it's about time you returned the compliment.'

'Why?' Cleo demanded. 'You can't possibly be interested in my problems.'

They were at the far end of the terrace now, quite alone and standing in semi-darkness, the only light coming from a nearby window.

'Then you are ready to admit that you have problems?' Maxim said, facing her.

Cleo realised at once that she had tumbled into a neat little trap.

'Everyone has problems,' she muttered at last. 'I'm sure mine aren't any worse than anyone else's.'

'Not worse,' agreed Maxim. 'But perhaps different.'

'What do you mean?' she said warily.

'There aren't very many beautiful twenty-three-year-old girls who don't like to be kissed.'

She was instantly on the defensive. 'Perhaps I just don't like being kissed by you!' she retorted.

'Maybe,' he said a little tightly. 'But I don't think so.'

'Because your kisses are so wonderful?' Cleo taunted him, ignoring the bright glitter which had suddenly appeared in his eyes. 'Well, I've got news for you,' she went on rashly. 'That kiss you gave me was very average. On a scale of one to ten, it rated about four to five. How do you like that?' she challenged him.

Perhaps the most frightening thing was the way Maxim remained in control of his temper. That really unnerved Cleo. Oh, yes, his eyes still glinted dangerously, but that was all. Nothing else betrayed what was really going on inside his head.

And he didn't say anything. Not a single word. She swallowed very hard, because she hadn't realised until now that silence could be such a potent weapon.

'Well, now we've got that sorted out, we'd better get back to the party,' she finally got out in a defiant tone.

'We haven't got anything at all sorted out. And we aren't going anywhere,' he told her levelly.

'You might not be, but *I* am,' she said, turning away from him.

His fingers instantly slid around her wrist. 'No, you're not.'

'Let go of me!' Cleo demanded at once.

'Not until I find out what's wrong.'

'There is *nothing* wrong,' she said stormily. 'Why won't you believe me?'

Without any warning, he bent his head and swiftly kissed her. The kiss lasted only a few seconds but, as always, she instinctively shrank back.

'When I kiss you, you behave like a frightened little mouse,' Maxim said in a rather grim tone. 'And don't try telling me again that you only behave like this with me, that you simply don't like my kisses. You don't like *anyone* kissing you, Cleo. *That's* your problem.'

She was trembling a little, now, but still defiant. 'I don't have to like being kissed,' she told him. 'I can live a perfectly happy, fulfilled life without kisses and—and any of those other things.'

'Love, sex, marriage, children? Yes, a lot of people can—and do—live without them. Some because they have no choice, some because it suits their nature, the kind of person that they are. But it doesn't suit you, Cleo. I think it's eating you up inside, making you so unhappy that it's ruining your life. But you don't know what to do about it, do you? You won't even admit that it's a problem, so how can you even ask for help?'

'I didn't come to this party to be psychoanalysed,' she said furiously. 'And you *don't* know any of those things about me, you're just guessing.'

'And have I guessed wrong?' Maxim said, his dark eyes locking on to her face.

'Yes!' she lied. 'My life is fine, I don't want to change one single thing about it. Anyway, I don't think you should be lecturing me about the way I live,' she rushed on. 'Your life isn't exactly perfect. You made a real mess of your marriage. And because you're like all men, you hate making mistakes, you don't even want to try again. It doesn't matter that William and Alice would be better off with a mother, as well as a father. You like your life exactly the way it is, and you've no intention of changing it. You accused me once of being selfish and self-centred, but you're exactly the same!'

Warning lines registered very clearly at the corners of Maxim's eyes and mouth.

'What do you want me to do?' he demanded softly. 'Go straight back inside and propose to Jane Templeton?'

Just the thought of him doing such a thing made Cleo suddenly feel very odd inside. With a deep shiver, she pushed the sensation away, and then tried to pretend she hadn't even felt it. She didn't care who this man married, she told herself fiercely. It wasn't anything to do with her, he could propose to half a dozen women and it wouldn't affect her *in the least*.

'Yes, go and propose to Jane,' she challenged him recklessly.

'You want me to live with someone I don't want, don't love, simply so my children can have a mother?' he said incredulously.

'Why not?' she said stubbornly. 'You're always saying that your children come first, that you only want what's best for them.'

'And you think it would be good for them to live in a household where there's no love? Just two people living a marriage of convenience?'

'I'm sure that Jane loves you.'

'Jane doesn't even know me,' Maxim said tautly. 'She doesn't have any idea of the kind of man I am. You know me better than she does.'

That threw Cleo right off balance. 'I—I can't know you better,' she stuttered. 'I've only been here a couple of days.'

'How long does it take to get to know someone?'

They were moving on to dangerous ground here. Cleo quickly stepped back.

'I've no idea,' she declared. 'And I don't really care. Look, I've had enough of this conversation. In fact, I've had enough of this damned party! I want to go home.'

To her surprise—and relief—Maxim didn't argue. Perhaps he, too, didn't want to take this any further.

'We can leave straight away, if that's what you really want,' he growled.

'It is!' she said with some vehemence. Then she turned round and stalked back into the house, without even looking to see if Maxim was following.

In fact, he was only one step behind her. She knew that without even turning around. She could sense the closeness of that powerful body, even seemed to be aware of that quick, probing mind.

She walked through the Templetons' house with her head held high, smiling blankly at people, and praying that her face didn't look too flushed, or her eyes too bright. If they did, then everyone would assume that she and Maxim were going home early for a very different reason!

Then Sarah came into sight. She waved to Cleo, and quickly walked over. 'Leaving already?' she said in some surprise. Then she looked at Cleo's face. A second later, her gaze fixed on her brother, who was still just a stride behind. 'Have you been behaving yourself, Maxim?' she said suspiciously.

'You know me,' Maxim said smoothly. 'Always the perfect gentleman.'

'Yes, I do know you,' his sister said promptly. Then she turned to Cleo. 'Is everything OK?'

'Everything is fine,' Cleo said in a tight voice.

Sarah sighed. 'I think that the two of you are telling whopping great lies. You're both too old for me to lecture you, though, so you'd better go home and sort it out between you. I'll see you in a couple of days.'

Once Cleo was in Maxim's car and heading away from the Templetons' house, she began to relax very slightly. Not long now, and this endless evening would be over. The car purred quietly through the village, where a few people were spilling out of the small pub and heading home, a couple of dogs were getting a late walk, and a group of teenagers sat on a low wall, earnestly discussing something. The more Cleo saw of the village, the more she liked the look of it. It was a comfortable, homely place, and she hoped she would get to know some of the people before it was time for her to go back to London.

Because she was wrapped up in her own thoughts, Cleo didn't immediately realise that Maxim had smoothly swung the car left and taken the road that led down towards the lake. When it finally dawned on her that they were going the wrong way, though, she sat bolt upright in alarm.

'What are you doing?'

'Just taking a temporary diversion.'

'I want to go straight back to the house,' she said at once.

'But I don't,' Maxim said calmly.

It took only a few seconds to reach the end of the short road. Maxim brought the car to a halt, cut the engine, and then got out. Cleo frowned at him. What was he up to now?

He walked the few yards down to the edge of the lake, and then simply stood there. She watched him for a while longer, then gave a small sigh of impatience and walked over to join him.

'Why are we here?' she said a little irritably.

'Because, at night, it's one of the most beautiful places in the world,' he said, to her astonishment.

Cleo looked around. He was right. The lake was mirror-smooth, reflecting the subtle silver light of the moon, and the darker shadows that gathered around the shores. The mountains rose up behind it like sleeping giants, with small pinpoints of yellow from the lit windows of houses nestling into their lower slopes. Overhead, stars shimmered in a dark velvet sky, and an owl hooted mournfully, repetitively in the distance.

'I wish my father could see this,' she said without thinking.

Maxim's dark brows drew together slightly. 'Don't you ever stop thinking about him?' he growled.

Cleo was rather startled by his response. 'I only meant that this quietness and tranquillity would be good for him. He's been working very hard lately. And when I last phoned him, he sounded a little odd, not really like himself at all. I really should ring him again,' she added, biting her lip. 'I'm not usually out of touch for this long.'

'Cleo, he is a mature, intelligent adult,' Maxim said with clear exasperation. 'He can cope for a few days without you.'

'Yes, of course he can,' she said, although not with a great deal of conviction. 'But he gets lonely. We've only got each other.'

'But it shouldn't be like that,' he pointed out. 'Why can't you see that the two of you are leading unnatural lives? I can understand that you needed to be close to him when you were a child, but it's time it stopped; you're too old to live like this any longer.'

'I don't think you've got any right to tell me how to live,' she said indignantly.

'Someone has to, since you obviously can't see it for yourself. It's no longer a healthy relationship, Cleo. And it's stopping *you* from becoming an independent adult and having a close relationship with anyone else.'

'I'm not interested in other relationships!' she said furiously.

'That should tell you that something's wrong, because you *should* be. You can't stay a little girl, indulged and spoilt, for the rest of your life.'

'Don't say those things!' she yelled at him. 'I think that you're just taking it out on me because I've got a loving parent, and you resent that. You're jealous, because all you had was a father who tried to dominate you all the time and a mother who neglected you!'

Maxim's face set into dark, furious lines. 'How dare you say something like that to me?'

'Why not?' she threw back at him, far more bravely than she felt. 'It's the truth, isn't it? I had a happy childhood, with everything that money could buy. And that's too much for you to stomach, isn't it?'

'Well-paid nursemaids and nannies, expensive toys, exclusive schools—do you think those are the things that make a happy childhood?' Maxim said cuttingly.

'Yes,' she said staunchly. 'When you're given all those things with love. But you don't understand love, do you? Perhaps that was your mother's fault, she didn't teach you the meaning of the word. Maybe that was why you made such a mess of your marriage!'

Cleo knew that she had gone too far. Even before she saw the icy anger in Maxim's eyes, she knew it.

'If I were a violent man, I would probably knock you to the ground right now,' he said in a taut, dangerous voice.

'I'm—I'm sorry,' she said in a more subdued tone. 'I shouldn't have said that.'

'No, you shouldn't,' he agreed, his eyes still glittering coldly. 'But since you've brought up the subject of love, Cleo, let's find out why someone who was supposedly given so much of it in her childhood is so scared of it now.'

'I'm not scared,' she insisted.

'Yes, you are. Scared to death. Scared even of a simple thing like a kiss.'

'I can manage a kiss,' Cleo declared at once, without stopping to think what she was saying.

Maxim's expression changed, he moved nearer, and her legs immediately began to shake. Too late, she realised that she shouldn't have said that. What if he wanted her to prove her words?

Maxim advanced still further, until he was only inches away. Cleo licked her lips. 'Let's go back to the car,' she said in a wary voice.

'Not yet. Before we go anywhere, I want you to convince me that you're not scared of physical contact. Give me just one kiss that you actually enjoy, Cleo.'

'I don't want to give you anything,' she said at once.

'I know that,' Maxim said, his dark eyes fixing on her, the intensity of his gaze somehow being enough to stop her from retreating. 'But that's what you've got to do, if you want to prove that you know anything at all about love. That is what this conversation has been about, hasn't it?' he challenged her softly. 'Which of us knows more about it?'

She couldn't retreat, the lake was behind her. And there was such a relentless look in Maxim's eyes, she had never seen him look quite like that before. He wasn't going to let her run away until this was over.

Cleo gave an exaggerated sigh, and hoped he couldn't hear how shakily it came out. 'All right,' she agreed. 'One kiss. And when I've proved to you that I'm quite capable of enjoying it, you'll let me go?' she added warily. She certainly didn't want this to go any further.

'You can run as far and as fast as you like.' His mouth came nearer and Cleo felt her stomach contract. You *can* do this, she told herself staunchly. Just a few seconds of pretence, that was all it would take. She had done it before, when she had been out on a date. She could do it again.

Maxim's lips closed over hers, their touch unexpectedly light; she had been expecting a hard, demanding kiss and had braced herself against. This was easy, she told herself with growing confidence. No problem at all. She politely kissed him back, and even managed to stay relaxed while she was doing it.

A few seconds later, Maxim released her. Cleo gave a silent sigh of relief. It was over, and she was sure that she had given a very credible performance.

'Did you enjoy that?' Maxim enquired.

'It was very nice,' she told him coolly.

'Liar,' he said at once in a flat voice, shocking her out of her complacency. 'You were faking it, I didn't get one ounce of genuine enjoyment or response out of you, Cleo.' His dark eyes narrowed, and his voice became a little grim. 'What happened to make you like this? A bad experience with a man? Someone treated you roughly, perhaps even assaulted you?'

'I've never had a bad experience,' she said at once, rather indignantly. 'I'd never let anyone treat me like that.'

'Women don't always get a choice, especially if the man is physically powerful.' Then some of the grimness left his voice, and his face became more thoughtful. 'No, I got it wrong, didn't I?' he said more slowly. 'Not a bad experience, Cleo. But no experience at all. That's it, isn't it?' he said with growing certainty. 'Too scared even to try.'

'That's—that's nonsense,' she insisted, shaken to the roots of her soul by the accuracy of his guess.

Maxim ran his hand slowly up her bare arm, over her shoulder, and then let his fingers linger around the nape of her neck. Her skin tingled under his touch. It wasn't an unpleasant sensation—not unpleasant at all. Cleo swallowed hard, and tried to remind herself that men rarely wanted to stop at just touching.

'That perfect body,' he said softly. 'It's hard to believe that it's untouched. A little too thin, but still very supple, very sensual. Do you know just how sensual you are, Cleo? Or is that something else that you never let yourself think about?'

She tried to say something, but her throat had suddenly gone too dry.

'You still haven't told me why,' he went on, and his voice was just like velvet, it stroked her as softly as his fingers, which were now caressing their way gently across her skin. 'But perhaps that isn't important for now. But you do know, Cleo, that you can't go on like this?'

She finally found her voice. 'Why—why not?' she croaked. 'I've managed very well until now.'

'No, you haven't,' Maxim told her. 'You're only just holding things together. You're too brittle, too tense, you're going to fly apart if you go on like this for much longer.'

He bent his head, and his mouth caressed against her skin, instead of his fingers. 'It really isn't so frightening,' he murmured. His fingertips touched her mouth, lightly ran around the perfect outline, her lips parted involuntarily, and she couldn't quite believe that she was standing here and letting him do this.

Maxim slid his fingers away and she found that, astonishingly, she missed them. But then his mouth took their place, he was kissing her again, and this time she *was* enjoying it, the warmth and the closeness, the gentle heat that was rising somewhere inside her own body, the awareness of an answering heat in his own. The kiss deepened, intensified, and still she didn't freeze up. Cleo couldn't understand it. Her mouth moved under his with an eagerness that was entirely new to her; she wanted it to go on and on, as if to make up for all the kisses that had been missing in her life until now.

Maxim's hand slid down, rested against the softness of her breast and she gave a small gulp. Oh, yes, she liked that, she liked it *very* much. And her body grew hotter, her breathing was a little quicker, and she had never felt quite like this before, except sometimes in confused, restless dreams.

Then Maxim let go of her, his mouth and his hands released her, and Cleo blinked, not quite understanding what was happening.

'Enough for now,' he told her, his own breathing not quite steady. 'This is something that needs to be taken one step at a time.'

Cleo slowly returned to reality. And as she did so, she was aware of a growing alarm and horror, because she knew where those seductive kisses had been slowly leading her. Towards a place that she had decided long ago she never wanted to go.

'That was the first and *last* step,' she told Maxim in a very stiff voice. 'This is never going to happen again!'

'Of course it is,' he told her calmly. 'If not with me, then with someone else. Time to grow up, Cleo. Time to stop being Daddy's little girl and join the real world, the adult world.'

And Cleo shivered, because that was just about the most frightening thing she could think of.

CHAPTER SEVEN

WHEN they got back to the house, Cleo went straight to her rooms in the annexe, stripped off the fuchsia-pink dress, kicked off her sandals, had a quick shower and then crawled into bed. Then she found that she couldn't sleep a single wink.

Every time she thought of that kiss, she shivered; then, when she thought of the way Maxim had touched her, she would shiver all over again. And the *really* scary part was how much she had liked it. If Maxim wanted to do the same thing again, then she wasn't at all sure she would try very hard to stop him...

But whenever those thoughts began to run through her head, she would run headlong into the old problem. Kisses and caresses might be very nice—much nicer than she had expected—but they led down a path that she was still far too terrified to take. With lovemaking, no matter how careful you were, there was always the risk of pregnancy. And the ghost of her dead mother still haunted Cleo's mind; she had lived with it for so many years that she had no idea how to exorcise it.

Dawn finally came and she got up, heavy-eyed and exhausted. Another shower slightly refreshed her, but there were shadows under her eyes that needed to be disguised with a light, skilful touch of make-up, and a drawn look to her face that no cosmetics could completely hide.

To her relief, William and Alice chattered brightly all through breakfast, which meant that she didn't have to bother too much with conversation. After they had finished eating and gone out into the garden to play, though, she was left alone with Maxim.

'I want to work on your portrait this morning,' he told her, as he stacked the plates into the dishwasher. 'You'd better go and change into the clothes you were wearing before.'

'I—I don't feel much like sitting this morning,' Cleo said hesitantly. 'Couldn't we leave it until some other time?'

'No,' he said flatly. 'Go and get changed, Cleo, and be in the studio in five minutes.'

It was somehow impossible to argue with him when he used that particular tone of voice. Cleo gave a deep sigh, went back to the annexe to pull on the dark leggings and purple T-shirt she had worn for the last sitting, and then made her way to the studio.

She settled herself into the chair by the window, and then waited apprehensively. She was absolutely certain that Maxim was going to want to talk about last night.

He didn't say a word, though. He expertly mixed paints on his palette and then worked in silence, pausing only to glance intently in her direction every now and then. After a while, Cleo slowly began to relax. It was obvious that he was concentrating solely on the work in hand; he didn't intend to discuss anything in the least personal.

After a while, she relaxed still further. The early autumn sunshine shone through the window, soft and golden, her heavy eyelids began to droop shut, and then she fell asleep.

When she opened her eyes again, she blinked dozily a couple of times and couldn't immediately remember where she was. Then her gaze fixed on Maxim, who was cleaning his brushes, and she remembered *everything*.

She sat bolt upright and nervously chewed her bottom lip. 'How long have I been asleep?' she asked.

'A couple of hours,' Maxim told her.

'A couple of hours?' she repeated in disbelief. 'Why didn't you wake me up?'

His eyes briefly gleamed. 'I assumed you'd had a restless night and needed the sleep.'

'I slept very well, thank you,' she lied in a stiff voice. She was *not* going to admit that a couple of kisses from him could keep her awake for all those long, dark hours.

'I want to ask you a favour,' Maxim went on.

'What kind of favour?' she asked very warily.

'Would you mind looking after William and Alice for a couple of hours this evening? There's a meeting in the village hall about the proposed development, and I promised Sarah that I'd pick up a couple of elderly people who want to go, but don't have transport. And I'll probably stay on for the meeting afterwards, to give Sarah some support. Usually, Mrs Branson babysits for me, but she wants to go to the meeting herself, so I told her that I'd try and find someone else.'

'No, I don't mind at all,' Cleo said at once. 'Is the meeting important?'

Maxim shrugged. 'It'll be a chance for the local people to let the developers know that they're solidly against their proposed plans. A representative of the development company will be there, to try and convince everyone that holiday cottages will be a huge benefit for the community. He won't succeed, of course, but these formalities have to be gone through.' He stood back from the canvas, looked at it critically for a few moments, and then threw a cloth over it. 'That's it for today. I've another painting to work on this afternoon. Lizzie's coming for one last sitting, so I can finish the last canvas for the exhibition.'

'The series of nudes?' she said, remembering. Then her brows creased slightly. 'But where do you keep them? There are only a couple of canvases down here.'

'I've another studio upstairs.'

'You've got *two* studios?'

'Why not? This is a big house, with plenty of rooms.'

'Can I look at the paintings?' Cleo blurted out the request, without really thinking what she was saying. 'No, that's all right,' she added hurriedly, 'I don't suppose you want anyone to see them before the exhibition.'

'You can take a look at them—if you want to,' Maxim said, looking directly at her.

'Well—all right,' she said, rather uncertainly. She was beginning to think that this wasn't a good idea, but it was rather too late to back out now.

She followed Maxim up the stairs and realised that this was the first time she had been in the upper part of the house. A long gallery stretched right along the front of the house, with wide windows giving stupendous views over the lake and the mountains. Several doors opened off the other side of the gallery, and Maxim stopped in front of one of them.

'This is my other studio,' he said, and he opened the door for her.

Cleo stepped inside, and then caught her breath. Paintings were stacked up against every available inch of wall space. Half a dozen of them were portraits in varying stages of completion, but the rest were the nude studies. And in the light that streamed in through the big windows, skin gleamed, hair shone, eyes sparkled with life. Not all of the women Maxim had painted were beautiful, some were plump, others were older, but all of them glowed with some special quality that Maxim had found in them, and transferred on to the canvas.

And they were marvellously sensual women. Proud of their bodies, even though they weren't perfect, not caring in the least that they didn't conform to the conventional idea of beauty. 'Here I am,' they seemed to say, 'take me, admire me, love me exactly the way I am.'

Cleo was awestruck. She had never seen paintings quite like these before. And she realised something else. Maxim's own passions might be tightly locked up inside of him, but when he picked up a brush he released them into his paintings.

Then she came to the last painting, and a huge wave of shock hit her. She briefly closed her eyes, but when she opened them again she found herself still staring at a painting of a woman who was not only nude, but heavily pregnant.

The woman looked totally relaxed, sitting in a chair with a couple of cushions to support her back, and her hands clasped over the great swell of her stomach, as if she were hugging her unborn child. She was smiling lazily, and seemed quite unconcerned about her very advanced state of pregnancy.

'How—how could you paint someone like that?' Cleo said in a choked voice.

Maxim moved over to stand behind her. 'That's Annabelle,' he said, in a relaxed voice. 'It was touch and go whether I could finish the painting before she gave birth. I actually made it with two days to spare. That bulge is now a very healthy boy called Sam.'

'I don't know how *anyone* could let themselves be seen like that,' Cleo said tightly. 'And what about her husband? That's hardly the kind of painting anyone would want of their wife!'

'Her husband actually commissioned the painting. He thought that his wife looked very beautiful while she was pregnant. So do I.'

Cleo didn't know what to say. She couldn't seem to look away from the painting; it repulsed and yet fascinated her. And she couldn't get over the way that the woman looked so at ease, as if her swollen stomach were entirely natural, and certainly nothing to be afraid of.

'I still want to include you in the collection,' Maxim told her softly, moving a little closer. 'Wearing that leotard. Nude, and yet not nude.'

She bit her lip. She knew now that there would be nothing embarrassing about being painted like that; these women had such an innocent sensuality, and the paintings weren't erotic, except perhaps in the very purest sense of the word. But she was still too shocked by that last painting to be able to think very straight.

'I—don't know,' she whispered at last.

'Think about it,' he said quietly. 'Let me know when you make up your mind.' Then he glanced at his watch. 'Lizzie will be here in a few minutes. Do you want to stay and watch me work?'

'No, I——' She swallowed rather hard, and then went on more firmly, 'I don't think so. I'm going to relax and sunbathe in the garden for a couple of hours.'

'Still not comfortable with naked bodies?' he said with a touch of amusement. 'Perhaps we'll be able to cure that before you leave here, Cleo. In fact, we might be able to cure you of quite a lot of things,' he added, in a very different tone of voice.

Her old defensiveness automatically sprang back into place. 'Thank you, but I don't need to be cured of anything,' she said in a stilted voice. Then she hurriedly retreated from the studio in case Maxim decided to try and convince her to the contrary.

She was worried that he might follow her, but relaxed again as she met Lizzie rushing up the stairs.

'Nice to see you again,' said Lizzie, rather breathlessly. 'Can't stop and chat, I'm late, and Mr Brenner hates unpunctuality.'

She dashed on up to the studio, and Cleo went down to the kitchen, where she made herself a pile of sandwiches and took them out into the garden, to eat them.

William and Alice were running around, playing a noisy, boisterous game, and she sat and watched them while she ate. Children were marvellously inventive, she decided after a while. Give them an overgrown garden, and they could turn it into just about anything they wanted. At the moment, it was apparently a desert island with wild animals, fierce natives, a swamp, several caves and a box of buried treasure. It didn't seem to matter that William and Alice couldn't actually see any of those things, they existed in their imagination, and that was enough.

When they finally got tired of that game, they came and flopped down beside Cleo for a while. They chatted about school, their friends, what they had done on holiday with Sarah and her family. Then they were up and off again, and another game got under way.

Cleo found it hard to take her eyes off them, they were so amazingly like Maxim to look at, with their dark eyes, black hair and strong bodies. She briefly wondered if Maxim's wife had found that a little heartbreaking, that they seemed to have inherited nothing from her.

The afternoon passed quickly and pleasantly. When the sun finally began to sink down in the sky, Maxim came out into the garden.

'I'm going down to the village now, for the meeting,' he told Cleo, 'but I shouldn't be more than a couple of hours. You're sure you don't mind looking after William and Alice?'

'No, I don't mind at all. We'll all be fine.'

The children came running over at that point. 'We're hungry,' announced William.

'They haven't had their tea,' Maxim said, with a small frown. 'Can you do something about that?'

Before Cleo could say anything, the two children rolled their eyes expressively. Their father shot them a warning look. 'Whatever Cleo gives you, you will eat,' he told them sternly.

'Even if it's poison?' said William, writhing on the ground and clutching his stomach expressively.

'William, stand up,' ordered Maxim.

William immediately got to his feet, and looked rather sheepish. 'I want both of you to behave yourselves,' their father said, looking directly at each child in turn. 'After tea, you can watch television or read for an hour. Then it's straight up to bed.'

Both children nodded solemnly. Then they obediently followed Cleo into the kitchen.

'Right,' she said, turning to face them, 'what do you want to eat? And if either of you says beefburgers, there will be trouble,' she added with mock severity.

They finally settled on chips and fish fingers, followed by ice cream. 'I don't want to watch television or read,' William announced, when he had finished eating. 'Can we go down to the village and see where Daddy's gone to the meeting?'

'Well—I don't see why not,' said Cleo. A walk would probably do them good, she decided. They would be able to let off some energy before going to bed. 'You won't be able to go in, though,' she warned.

'That's all right. We can just have a look, and then come home again.'

She despatched them up to their rooms, to find light jackets in case the evening grew cool. Then they all trooped out of the house and headed across the fields, towards the village.

William and Alice ran on ahead, while Cleo followed at a more sedate pace. Dusk was beginning to fall, but she was confident that they had plenty of time to get back to the house before night set in.

When they reached the village, it seemed completely deserted. Everyone must be at the meeting, Cleo decided. Sarah would be pleased that so many people had turned up to support her.

The hall was at the far end of the village. There were a lot of cars packed around it, and Cleo realised that people must have come from far and wide to attend this meeting.

'Well, this is it,' she said to William and Alice. Then she looked at them. 'Do you know why everyone's come here tonight?'

'Of course,' Alice said at once. 'They want to build houses where people can go on holiday, but Auntie Sarah's going to make them build houses that people can live in. And Daddy's helping her.'

Cleo grinned. 'That's about it,' she agreed. Then she looked at her watch. Time to go back to the house and persuade William and Alice that it was time to go to bed.

As she started to turn away, though, one of the cars parked outside the hall suddenly caught Cleo's eye. It stood out from all the other, more ordinary cars like a sore thumb. Big, gleaming and very expensive, it also had a distinctive number plate that Cleo was sure she recognised.

'What is it?' asked Alice, tugging at her hand.

'That car,' said Cleo thoughtfully, 'the big silver one—I think it belongs to Gordon Hamilton.'

'Who's he?'

'Someone my father knows. He's been to our house a couple of times, for dinner.'

And Cleo had disliked him instantly. He was a big, overbearing man, whose sole interest in life seemed to be the pursuit of profit. He had continually boasted about the deals he had made, and the promises he had made to secure those deals. Then he had found clever ways of breaking those same promises once the deal had gone through. He was powerful and very formidable, though, and if he was in charge of the proposed development, then Sarah might well find that she had a much harder fight ahead on her hands than she had expected.

She led William and Alice to a small clump of trees just behind the hall. 'Look, I want to peep through the window, to see if it *is* Gordon Hamilton in that hall. I want you to wait right here, well away from the cars. I'll only be a minute, and you'll be able to see me all the time. All right?'

William nodded, and Alice didn't seem at all worried about being left with her brother for a very short time. Cleo quickly walked over to the nearest window, and tried to see inside the hall. The window was misted up, though, and she gave a small frown as she realised that she couldn't see clearly.

There was another window a little further down, and she decided to try that one. If she still couldn't see, then she would just have to give up.

She had just reached the second window when she heard a sudden scream from Alice, followed almost at once by a worried shout from William. Cleo spun round and looked anxiously in their direction. What was going on?

Then she saw Alice lying in a small, crumpled heap at the foot of one of the trees. Cleo's heart almost seemed to stop beating. Then she was racing over to the ominously still figure of the child.

'What happened?' she gasped to William, as he stared down at his sister.

'Alice tried to climb the tree,' he said in a small voice. 'And she fell.'

As Cleo looked at Alice's white face and closed eyes, she knew that she had never been so frightened in her entire life. There was a small trickle of blood on the child's forehead, and as Cleo very, very carefully explored with her fingers, she could feel a large bump already swelling up.

Cleo fought back a huge wave of panic. She had to think straight, she had to *do* something.

'Alice needs to see a doctor,' she said rapidly to William. 'Is there one in the village?'

'I—I don't know,' he stuttered, looking almost as panic-stricken as she did.

She took a very deep breath and caught hold of his hands, trying to steady him as well as herself.

'All right, William, this is what we'll do,' she said in what she hoped was a calming voice. 'I'll stay here with Alice, and you go into the meeting and fetch your father.'

He immediately looked relieved. 'Yes, Daddy will make Alice better,' he said with new confidence, and he dashed off.

Cleo gazed at Alice again, and felt her stomach clench with an almost unbearable tension. She was terrified that the small girl might have hurt herself very badly, and absolutely petrified of facing Maxim. He had left his two children in her care, and now one of them was injured, and it was all *her* fault.

She stroked Alice's dark hair and then held her hand, as if to reassure the unconscious child that someone was with her, she wasn't on her own. Then Cleo raised her head and saw Maxim running towards them.

When she saw his face, her heart pounded away even more furiously. She had never seen him—never seen *anyone*—look quite like that before.

He dropped to his knees beside his daughter, and then looked grimly up at Cleo. 'How did this happen?' he demanded.

In halting sentences, she told him, as he ran his hands carefully over Alice's small body, searching for any injuries that weren't immediately visible. When she finally finished speaking, Maxim raised his head, and she saw that his dark eyes were blazing with utter fury.

'You went off and left two small children on their own?' he roared at her. 'How dare you do something like that?'

Cleo tried to gabble some sort of desperate apology, but Maxim wasn't even listening. Instead, he was gathering Alice up into his arms and calling to William. Then he strode quickly towards his car.

She hurried after him. William scrambled into the front, while Maxim very carefully laid Alice on the back seat. Then he turned round, caught hold of Cleo and unceremoniously bundled her into the back beside Alice.

'Hold her as carefully as you can, so that she isn't bumped around too much while I'm driving,' he instructed grimly. Then he got into the front, revved the engine up, and drove off swiftly but very smoothly.

The large, powerful car purred along the narrow roads, eating up the miles. Darkness was falling swiftly now, but Maxim didn't decrease his speed.

'Where are we going?' Cleo asked in a shaken voice, after a while.

'To the nearest hospital,' he replied curtly, and didn't say another word, giving all of his concentration to the unlit road ahead.

To Cleo it seemed forever before the car finally pulled up outside a large building that was obviously a hospital, although it was probably not more than quarter of an hour. Maxim drove directly up to the front entrance, jumped out and gently picked up Alice. Then he strode inside, with William running after him.

Cleo stayed in the car and gently shivered, mainly because she was so frantically worried about Alice, but also because she was so near to a hospital—the one place on earth where she never wanted to be.

She had no idea how long she waited in the car. Part of her wanted to run and keep on running, away from this place of illness and death. She stayed exactly where she was, though, not moving and breathing only shallowly. Time seemed to have become quite meaningless. Finally, though, the door opened again and Maxim's tall, dark figure appeared. All of Cleo's nerves jumped violently and she licked her bone-dry lips.

Maxim walked over to the car and opened the door. Then he slumped tiredly into the seat beside her.

'Alice——?' Cleo managed to get out in a quavery voice, not able to say anything more than just that one word.

'She's conscious, she's got a headache, but apart from that she's fine,' he said, his own voice sounding utterly drawn. 'The doctors have X-rayed and examined her, and they can't find any serious or permanent damage. They're going to keep her in overnight, just as a precaution, but she can come home tomorrow morning as long as there aren't any complications.'

Cleo felt giddy with relief. 'Oh, God, I'm so glad,' she said thankfully. 'I was so worried——'

'Worried about Alice?' Maxim cut in more grimly. 'Or of what I would say—or do—to you?'

'Both,' she admitted. 'I know how you feel about your children, I just didn't know how to face you, what to say to you, after letting something like this happen to one of them.'

'When I first saw Alice lying there, I wanted to kill you,' he said slowly. 'But I've been talking to William while we were waiting for the results of the X-rays, and he's told me more about it. I know that you only left them on their own for a couple of minutes. And since you've had next to no contact with children, I suppose you couldn't be expected to know that that's all the time they need to get into trouble.'

'It was still all my fault,' Cleo said in a very subdued tone.

'Yes, a lot of it was your fault,' Maxim agreed. 'Leaving them on their own for even that short time was pretty irresponsible. William said you wanted to look through the windows of the hall. Why on earth did you want to do that?'

'I thought that I recognised one of the cars in the car park. You see, I think that I know who owns that car, he's a ruthless, devious man who'll use every under-handed trick in the book to get what he wants. Sarah needs to be warned about him.'

'I take it that you're talking about Gordon Hamilton?'

Cleo's eyes opened wide. 'You know him?'

'I certainly know about his reputation. And I've already given Sarah some suggestions on how to deal with him.'

'Oh,' she said, totally deflated. 'Then I wasn't even being helpful.'

'No. But you were trying, and I suppose that's a point in your favour.' Then he glanced at his watch. 'It's way past William's bedtime. I'd better get him home. He's had enough excitement for one day, he needs to get some sleep.'

'Where is he?' she asked.

'I left him with Alice, to keep her company while I came out to fetch you.'

'Fetch me?' she repeated uneasily.

'Alice wants to say goodnight to you. Just pop in and chat to her for a couple of minutes, and then tell her you'll see her again in the morning. The doctors don't want her to talk too much tonight, they want her to rest.'

Cleo bit her lip. 'No,' she said almost inaudibly. 'No, I can't do it.'

Maxim's black brows began to draw together. 'What are you talking about?'

'I can't—can't go in there.'

'Of course you can,' he said brusquely. 'Alice is waiting for you, she doesn't want to go to sleep until she's seen you.'

'I hate hospitals,' she burst out. 'I *hate* them.'

'A hospital is just a building,' Maxim said, his dark eyes fixing on her face. 'And I think that you owe it to Alice just to walk into that building for a couple of minutes, to say goodnight to her.'

Cleo felt herself go very hot, and then freezing cold, as if she had a sudden high fever. She hadn't been inside a hospital since her father had taken her on that last visit to see her mother, just before the baby had been stillborn and everything had gone so terribly wrong. She knew that Maxim was right, though. She had to do it, for Alice's sake.

As if sleepwalking, she got out of the car. Maxim was right beside her, still looking at her intently, as if trying to figure out what this was all about. Very slowly, she walked towards the hospital—no, towards the *building*, she told herself, that was all it was, a *building*, nothing to be frightened of.

She didn't know that she was white as a sheet, or that her green eyes were huge with fear. She did know that, as she went through the front doors, Maxim suddenly took hold of her hand, his fingers warm, hard and steadying.

'It isn't far,' he told her. 'Just along this corridor.'

Then he was opening a door, and there was Alice lying in bed, with William sitting beside her. She was still a little pale, but her dark eyes were open and bright and focused, and she smiled as Cleo walked in.

'Hello,' she said.

'Hello, sweetheart,' Cleo said in a shaky voice. 'How are you?'

'My head hurts a bit, but I'm all right really. I'm going to stay here tonight, the nurse is going to look after me and I can have the light on all night, if I want to. And I'm going to have breakfast in bed in the morning,' she said importantly. She was obviously beginning to look on it as a big adventure.

'That's enough talking, Alice,' her father said gently. 'Try and get some sleep. And we'll be here first thing in the morning, to take you home.'

'Don't come too early, Daddy,' she instructed. 'I want to have my breakfast in bed first.'

'If we get here too early, we'll wait while you finish breakfast,' he said drily. 'Stop chattering, Alice, and close your eyes.' He bent over and lightly kissed her. 'Goodnight, and sleep tight.'

'Goodnight, Alice,' Cleo added.

Alice yawned, suddenly looking tired. She curled up under the bedclothes, shut her eyes and was obviously already half asleep.

The three of them quietly left the room. Once they were outside, Cleo blinked, as if suddenly realising where she was. Sharp smells assaulted her, antiseptic, medical smells, and then a porter pushed a trolley by with a comatose patient on it. Her throat abruptly went dry. She was *inside* a hospital, and only the need to see Alice had got her here; but now Alice was asleep, safely tucked up in bed, and Cleo found herself surrounded by the sights, the sounds, the smells that she had avoided for so long, and she could feel the panic welling up inside of her, hot and uncontrollable. And Maxim was no longer holding her hand, there was nothing to cling on to, no hard warmth, this was *awful*, she really didn't think she could stand it...

A second later, Cleo fainted dead away.

CHAPTER EIGHT

WHEN Cleo came round, she discovered that she was sitting in Maxim's car. The window was wound down, so that the cool night air could drift in, and she felt very confused.

'What—what happened?' she croaked.

William, who was sitting in the front seat, swung round to face her.

'You fainted,' he announced. 'Everyone came rushing up and they all made a lot of fuss, but Daddy just picked you up and carried you out to the car.'

Cleo could feel herself going bright red. 'Sorry to cause so much bother,' she whispered.

'They wanted to keep you in for a couple of hours, to make sure you were all right,' Maxim told her. 'But I warned them that if you woke up and found yourself in a hospital bed you'd simply pass out all over again.'

She gave a small shudder at just the thought of being kept in hospital for a couple of hours.

'Girls always faint,' William said, with a frown. 'Why do they do that, Daddy?'

'Perhaps they're simply more sensitive than we are,' Maxim said, after a short pause.

'What does sensitive mean?' William demanded.

Maxim gave a weary shake of his head. 'No more questions tonight, William. Everyone's too tired to answer them.'

'I'm not tired,' William said promptly. 'I could probably go on asking questions all night.' Then, as he caught the warning gleam in his father's eyes, he slid down in his seat. 'But I probably won't,' he said, and sat very quiet and still for the rest of the drive back to the house.

After they went inside, Maxim took Cleo into the drawing-room, sat her down in a chair and then gave her a glass of brandy. 'Drink this and stay here,' he instructed. 'I'm taking William up to bed, but I'll be back and I want to talk to you.'

'I'm very tired,' she argued weakly.

'We're all very tired,' he said briefly. 'But this won't wait until morning.'

Cleo guessed that he wanted to talk about Alice, and what had happened this evening. She was probably in for another lecture. Perhaps he even wanted to order her to leave, although surely he wouldn't throw her out in the middle of the night? She couldn't be sure, though. Maxim was very protective of his children, perhaps he didn't want someone who had injured one of them staying under his roof for one minute longer.

She sipped the brandy, but it didn't really make her feel any better. She didn't know what *would* make her feel better. Something that would make her forget everything that had happened this evening, she supposed. But what could do that?

One of Maxim's kisses? The thought slid, unbidden, into her head, shocking her. Then the door opened and Maxim walked back in, sending another severe jolt through her already overloaded nervous system.

She licked her dry lips. 'About Alice——' she began.

'Alice is going to be fine,' he cut in. 'It could have turned out very badly, but it didn't, so let's leave it at that.'

'But you must blame me for what happened,' she insisted.

'You're inexperienced with children, you don't know what endless mischief they can get up to whenever your back's turned. In future you'll be more careful, so today has taught you a valuable lesson.'

'Then—you don't want me to leave?'

Maxim frowned. 'Leave? Of course not. But I do want to talk to you about something.'

'About what?' she said with some caution.

'This irrational fear you have of hospitals. What caused it? When did it start?'

Cleo immediately clammed up. She had never spoken about this to anyone. It was very personal, very private. Anyway, he didn't have any *right* to ask questions like that.

'I think that's my business,' she said as politely as she could. Then she got to her feet. 'It's been a very long, exhausting day, I'm going to bed now——'

In two strides, Maxim was standing in front of her. 'You're not going anywhere,' he told her. 'Not until you've told me what this is all about.'

Cleo's eyes briefly flashed. 'I don't have to tell you anything! Now, please get out of my way.'

He didn't move an inch. 'You're so scared of hospitals that just being in one for a few minutes tonight made you drop to the floor in a dead faint. Why, Cleo?'

'Lots of people don't like hospitals,' she retorted.

'But they don't react like that.' His dark eyes fixed intently on her face. 'Going to give me an answer?'

She didn't mean to say anything at all. Instead, to her astonishment, she found herself bursting out, 'It's just a phobia, I can't do anything about it!'

Maxim's gaze never wavered. 'Of course you can. Begin by talking about it, telling me what's made you so terrified of going into a hospital.' Then his eyes abruptly narrowed. 'No, I'm asking the wrong question, aren't I?' he went on more softly. 'Who did you lose in a hospital? That's the answer to this puzzle, isn't it?'

His perceptiveness shook her so thoroughly that her defences began to slip away.

'M-my mother,' she whispered, the words somehow being forced out of her, and she just couldn't stop them, she wasn't even sure that she *wanted* to stop them. 'She—she went into a hospital and never came home again.'

Maxim briefly frowned. 'Your mother died in a hospital? And you went to see her before she died?'

'Yes, only I can't remember it. At least, I remember the funny smells, and my father telling me that the doctors would soon make her better, but I can't remember her face, I wish that I could, but I just can't. And the next thing I remember is my father crying, I'd never seen him cry before, I didn't know that grown men cried, and he said—he said——' Her voice faltered, and then stopped.

'You thought that the hospital took her away from you?' Maxim said gently.

'I was only five at the time, that was certainly what I *did* think. And even though I'm old enough now to know that's nonsense, it's still all so mixed up inside my head, hospitals, childbirth, it all frightens me so much.'

'Childbirth?' Maxim queried a little sharply. 'Your mother went into hospital to have a baby?'

'Yes. Didn't I tell you that? There were complications, though. I don't know exactly what they were, my father would never talk about it, but something went awfully wrong, she and the baby both—both——' Her voice trailed away again for a minute. 'I've always had this awful fear that the same thing will happen to me,' she finally finished, almost inaudibly. 'I know that it isn't logical, but phobias don't make any sense, do they?'

'No,' he said after a short pause. 'No, they don't. Cleo, you should have talked to someone about this a long time ago. Got professional help. What happened to your mother was tragic, but you can't let it ruin *your* life, you can't live forever with this fear.'

'I've never been able to talk about it, not to anyone.'

'You're talking to me,' he said levelly. Then he caught hold of her and lightly shook her. 'That's what you need to do—keep talking.'

But she was already trying to pull away from him. 'Please—don't touch me,' she said jerkily.

'Because it's something else that you're frightened of? Because you know that touching leads to other things?' His dark eyes still hadn't left her face, that powerful gaze seemed to be seeing right inside her head. 'It's why you shrank back when I first kissed you, isn't it? Why you keep insisting that you don't want children? It's got nothing to do with wanting to keep that beautiful body of yours in perfect shape! You're just terrified of pregnancy and childbirth.' He shook his head slowly. 'You can't go on like this, Cleo.'

She raised her head and stared back at him with wide, vulnerable eyes. 'I don't know how to stop it,' she whispered.

The grip of his fingers increased, digging deeper into her silken skin.

'Try remembering that you're young and you're healthy; all the odds are against anything happening to you. And you also have to have the courage to take a few risks sometimes; you can't live forever in a safe little cocoon.'

'Why not?' she retorted, stung back into life by his unspoken accusation of cowardice. '*You* don't take risks, do you? Your marriage went wrong, so you won't try again, you run away from relationships. What's the difference between that and me running away from the risk of pregnancy, from giving in to my phobia about hospitals?'

For a moment, anger flashed brightly in his eyes. Then it gradually died away again. 'Maybe there's no difference at all,' Maxim said slowly, at last. 'Perhaps we should try and teach each other to take risks.'

'I—I don't think I want to do that,' she said unsteadily. Yet part of her did. Part of her wanted all the things she had never had, the things she had always denied herself; wanted the touch of his experienced hands, the warmth of his mouth against her lips, her skin. She had been starved of physical closeness for too long, she was starting to long for it with a terrifying intensity. But not with just anyone, it had to be with this man, Maxim Brenner, whom she had only known for a brief time, but who already knew most of her most closely guarded secrets.

Perhaps those last few thoughts had been written too clearly on her face. Maxim seemed to sense her weakness, for he was already moving closer, and she caught her breath as she felt the warmth of his body brushing against her.

'How much of a risk do you think we should take?' he asked in a voice that was suddenly husky. 'Perhaps just a small one, to start with,' he went on, answering his own question. 'Because neither of us have had much practice at this, have we?' Then his mouth skimmed over her own, light and yet highly arousing, and she could feel her lips trembling, wanting more of that sensual contact, and yet still scared of it.

She tried to push him away, but once her hands had touched him she simply wanted to feel him; heat was suddenly radiating out from her palms and her skin felt rawly sensitive. And his muscles involuntarily tensed under her touch, and an answering tremor ran over his own skin. A moment later, she drew her hand back again, alarmed at her behaviour. Don't do this, she warned herself. It isn't safe, isn't *safe*...

But she was so tired of being careful, of her restricted life, of living with all those inner fears; there had to come a time when it simply had to stop. And this man somehow, miraculously, made her feel as if that time could be now.

'Let me touch you,' Maxim murmured in her ear. 'Don't be afraid, I won't let this go too far, I know how scared it makes you. I simply want to touch...'

And she found herself relaxing against him as his fingers moved restlessly over her, skimming over delicate bones, lingering with restrained hunger against the soft curves of breast and hips, pulling her more closely against him so that she could feel his heat and hardness, then easing her away again before his breathing could quicken and run out of control.

He kissed her once, briefly, as if he knew that a longer kiss might put both of them in danger. Then he drew back, and looked down into her dilated green eyes.

'Enough for now,' he instructed softly. 'You're too exhausted, and I keep thinking about Alice, seeing her in that hospital bed. But soon, Cleo—soon——'

He bent his head, gave her one more swift, hard kiss, then turned round and left the room, walking very quickly as if he needed to get away from her while he still had the strength of mind to leave.

Cleo stumbled back to her own room, tired, confused, her body aching, her head spinning. Today had been the most turbulent day of her entire life. And tomorrow—she found that she didn't even dare think about tomorrow.

In the morning, though, she woke up feeling hot and yet shivery. Her head ached and she felt too exhausted even to crawl out of bed.

She knew at once what it was. It had happened to her before, when she had been through a period of great stress. She developed these flu-like symptoms, which lasted for several days, and then went as quickly as they had come.

Cleo gave a small groan. This was not a good time to be ill. She decided to try and sleep for a couple of hours. Perhaps when she woke up again, she would feel better.

She slept right through until midday, but felt just as bad when she next opened her heavy eyes. She was still lying there half an hour later, trying to summon up enough energy to get out of bed, when there was a knock on the door.

'Come in,' she croaked.

The door opened and William came in. When he saw her lying in bed, he gave a small frown.

'You should be up,' he said rather disapprovingly. 'Daddy sent me to tell you that dinner is ready. We're having spaghetti bolognese, because that's Alice's favourite.'

Cleo gave a small shudder as she mentally pictured a large plateful of spaghetti bolognese. Then she belatedly remembered that Alice was being allowed home from hospital today.

'Has your daddy been to fetch Alice?' she asked a little anxiously.

William nodded. 'She's in bed, she's got to stay there for a couple of days. Are *you* going to stay in bed, as well?' he said, with another frown.

'I'm not feeling well,' Cleo mumbled.

'It isn't much fun, with everyone in bed,' he grumbled.

'I'll get up as soon as I feel better,' Cleo promised. 'Just tell your daddy that I don't want anything to eat, but he's not to worry, I'll be all right soon.'

'All right, I'll tell him,' he said, and he skipped out the door.

Cleo closed her eyes and had just begun to doze when the door opened again. She gave a weary sigh. She really didn't think she was up to another conversation with William.

This time, though, it was Maxim who stood in the doorway. And he was looking at her with some concern. 'What's wrong with you?' he demanded.

'Nothing,' she said sleepily.

'Then why are you still in bed? And why did you tell William you were ill?'

She forced her eyes open again and tried to make her woozy mind work.

'Look,' she said, 'this is just something that happens when I get overstressed. I run a high temperature and feel as if I've got the flu. I have to stay in bed for a while, and when I do get up I feel flaked out for a few days. Then it goes and I'm perfectly OK again.'

'You'd better see a doctor,' Maxim said at once.

'I don't *need* a doctor. I've told you, it's happened before, it's nothing to worry about.'

'You're still going to see a doctor. As a matter of fact, he's coming round to check on Alice this afternoon. He can see you at the same time. Is there anything you need right now?'

'To be left in peace and quiet,' she said, rather ungratefully, and she pointedly closed her eyes again.

She slept until the arrival of the doctor. After giving her a thorough check-up, he confirmed her own diagnosis. There was nothing wrong with her that a few days of complete rest wouldn't cure. 'Some people react to stress like this,' he told Maxim briskly. 'They cope with it for a while, then they suddenly crack up.'

'I haven't cracked up,' Cleo mumbled, with a touch of annoyance.

'No, of course not,' said the doctor sympathetically, 'That was a poor choice of words. I simply meant that our bodies and minds sometimes decide that we need a rest. So they produce genuine symptoms of illness, forcing us to take a break. I'm coming to see Alice again in a couple of days, and I'll take another look at you afterwards. You'll probably be starting to feel a little better by then.'

In fact, it was three days before Cleo felt like getting out of bed. During that time, Maxim and William took it in turns to bring her drinks and small tempting plates of food, which she tried to eat. Even Alice came down in her nightdress, to chat for a few minutes before being shooed back to bed by Maxim.

Cleo found that she rather liked being pampered by the Brenners. And she *was* beginning to feel better, although she was still awfully tired all the time. The following Monday, William went back to school, although Alice was being kept home for a few more days. William thought that was very unfair, especially as his cousin,

Richard, was also still at home because of his chicken-pox. He walked around looking fairly thunderous until Cleo promised him that she would take him to school in her red sports car as soon as she felt well enough. That cheered him up, and he was singing tunelessly when Maxim took him to school the following morning.

Rather belatedly, Cleo remembered to ring her father, to let him know that she would be staying on for even longer than expected. Since she didn't want to worry or alarm him, she simply told him that she had a flu-like virus, but she was almost over it now. Rather to her surprise, he didn't sound too concerned. Once he had made sure that she was all right, he told her to stay on for as long as she liked. Then, without even telling her that he was missing her, he said goodbye and hung up. Cleo was rather surprised—and hurt—but told herself that he must still be working very hard. He simply hadn't had time to miss her.

For the next few days she and Alice both lazed around, reading books, watching television, or just chatting. And sometimes they would sit in Maxim's studio while he worked. Cleo would listen to music, while Alice painted small, smudgy pictures in bright colours. It was all very relaxing, and Cleo felt herself gradually beginning to return to her old self again. Alice, too, seemed to have completely recovered from her fall, and would be going back to school the following week.

Cleo realised that she was beginning to feel like one of the family. A small voice inside her head warned that it was very dangerous to feel like that, but she ignored it because she found that she liked their casual acceptance of her; she liked it very much. And with the days slipping lazily by it was all too easy to forget that things couldn't go on like this forever.

Saturday came round, and Cleo woke up feeling fine and full of energy. She spent the morning playing in the garden with the children, and then went into the kitchen to get them some lunch. Maxim came into the kitchen just as she was getting some pizzas out of the freezer. Her cooking was still at the very basic stage, and she wasn't ready to tackle anything too complicated yet.

'How do you feel today?' he asked casually.

'As if I could run a marathon,' she grinned. 'Why?'

'There's going to be a big protest march this afternoon against the proposed development. The press and TV cameras will be there, and Sarah's hoping it'll make the national news and daily papers. A few well-known faces at the front of the march could help to ensure that happens. I've managed to drum up a local author and an actor, and a beautiful model would look good alongside them, and help to draw the cameras.'

Cleo blinked. 'You mean me?'

'If you're feeling well enough, Sarah would certainly appreciate it.'

'Well—yes—OK, I'll do it,' she said.

'You won't have to walk too far,' Maxim told her. 'They're only marching from the village to the proposed site of the development. Sarah will make a short speech, everyone will clap like mad and then you can come home again.'

'Aren't you coming on the march?' she asked with a touch of disappointment.

'I've a client coming for a sitting this afternoon. I'll come and pick you up afterwards, though, in case the walk tires you more than you expect.'

'What time does the march start?'

'Two o'clock.' Maxim glanced at his watch. 'That gives you an hour and a half to have lunch, and get ready.'

Cleo gulped down her pizza, then shot off to the annexe. For the first time in a couple of weeks, she intended to go back to her 'model girl' look. Maxim wanted her to attract the attention of the cameras, and that was exactly what she intended to do!

She coaxed her hair into a dazzling riot of blonde curls, and made up her face with professional expertise, using just the minimum of make-up to emphasise her big green eyes, the fullness of her mouth, the perfection of her bone-structure. Then she pondered over what to wear. In the end, she pulled on jogging trousers and a matching sweatshirt, and wriggled her feet into a pair of old trainers. She might as well be comfortable, because some of the march was bound to be across rough ground.

When she finally left the annexe she found Maxim was standing in the hall. As she walked towards him, his dark eyes swept over her assessingly.

'Do I look OK?' she asked, slightly anxiously.

'You look fine,' he told her.

'I didn't know if I should wear something more dressy. I mean, the reason you want me on the march is to attract the attention of the cameras for publicity, isn't it?'

'Oh, I think you'll attract their attention,' Maxim said, his eyes taking on a much darker gleam.

For the first time in several days, Cleo felt her nerves give a hefty twitch. Since her illness, she had begun to feel so very relaxed with Maxim that she had almost forgotten how very *un*relaxed he could make her feel when his eyes glittered and his mouth set into that sensual line.

She hurriedly told herself that she really didn't have to worry about that last remark, or the gleam in his eyes. It was the weekend, and both William and Alice were at home all day. She was perfectly safe as long as they were around.

'Are you sure that you feel well enough to go through with this?' Maxim asked her, as she began to head towards the door.

'Yes, I really am,' she assured him.

'All the same, I'll come and pick you up at the end of the march,' he told her. 'You might feel a lot more tired than you expect.'

Cleo began to tell him that wasn't necessary, but he immediately held up his hand in a gesture that told her he didn't intend to argue about it. Then he left her, heading in the direction of his studio.

As she left the house, Cleo found herself wondering what would happen next week when Alice, as well as William, went back to school, leaving her alone in the house with Maxim. In the end she decided not to think about that. Anyway, now she was better again, Maxim could restart work on her portrait. It would soon bc finished, and then she could go home. The only trouble was, she was very aware by now that there was a large part of her that didn't want to go...

She tried to convince herself that she did want to go, told herself that she *had* to go home. Her father was waiting for her, lonely without her, she couldn't walk out and leave him. And, anyway, Maxim hadn't said that he wanted her to stay. And even if he had, how could she? He wouldn't be interested in a platonic friendship, he would want more from her, *much* more, and all the old familiar fears were still there, they weren't miraculously going to vanish...

Cleo was glad when she reached the large crowd of people thronging in the center of the village because it gave her something else to think about. Sarah soon caught sight of her, and came over.

'I'm really grateful you're doing this,' she exclaimed. 'Come and meet the rest of my family. And you haven't met my husband either, have you?'

Cleo found herself surrounded by four lively, yelling children, including Richard who was now over his chickenpox. Sarah's husband turned up a moment later, a very good-looking man with a wry grin.

'Hello,' he said. 'Good of you to come. I suppose Maxim talked you into it?'

'Well—yes. Although I'm happy to help, I think Sarah's right to protest about this development.'

'The Brenners are usually right about most things,' he said, with a resigned shake of his head. 'And Sarah's still very much a Brenner, even though she's been married to me for nearly nine years.' He was obviously proud of his wife, though, and he was soon helping her to sort out the crowd of people into an orderly column.

The protest march finally set off, with Cleo walking at the very front, flanked by Sarah and her family on one side, and the actor and author that Maxim had persuaded to join the march on the other. The TV cameras were there, and they lingered for a long time on the dazzlingly photogenic image that Cleo projected, while flashbulbs popped incessantly as the Press hustled each other for close-up pictures.

When they finally reached the development site, Sarah made a short but powerful speech, setting out clearly and cogently the reasons for their opposition to the plans. There was a great roar of approval when she had finally finished speaking, and then the crowd of people slowly began to break up.

Sarah looked flushed and excited. 'I think that went very well, don't you?' she said, coming over to rejoin her family and Cleo. 'Are you going to walk back with us, Cleo?' she added.

'No, Maxim's coming to pick me up,' she said. 'I'd better wait for him.'

'See you in a couple of days, then. And thanks again for supporting us.'

Cleo sat down on a nearby patch of grass, enjoying the last of the late afternoon sunshine as she waited for Maxim. He arrived ten minutes later, and she got into the car.

'Hungry?' he asked her.

'Starving,' she said at once.

'Then we'll go and have dinner somewhere, before going back to the house.'

'What about William and Alice?'

'Mrs Branson is babysitting for a couple of hours.'

He took her to a small restaurant in Ambleside, where they had a long, leisurely meal. Neither of them talked very much, but Cleo felt surprisingly relaxed. Or perhaps she was just tired, after the excitement of the march.

By the time they finally drove back to the house, night had fallen. As they got out of the car and she walked towards the house, she suddenly realised there were no lights on.

'Why is the house so dark?' she asked, puzzled.

'Because it's empty,' he replied calmly.

'Empty?' Cleo echoed, a little suspiciously. 'But William and Alice——'

'I asked Mrs Branson to take them over to Sarah's, when she'd given them their tea,' he told her. 'They'll be staying there overnight.'

'Why didn't you tell me about this arrangement?' she demanded.

'There's nothing unusual about it,' Maxim replied in an unruffled voice. 'They often stay at Sarah's house over the weekend.' Then he opened the door and went inside.

Cleo followed him more slowly. The house seemed very quiet and empty without the children. And still dark—Maxim hadn't switched on any lights.

She hurriedly clicked down the nearest switch, but nothing happened.

'Why don't the lights come on?' she asked, beginning to feel more than a little unnerved.

'Must be a power failure,' Maxim said, sounding quite unconcerned. 'It happens sometimes. Wait here, and I'll find some candles.'

But Cleo couldn't help worrying. The dark house, no children around—and because she couldn't see Maxim's face, she couldn't tell what was going on inside his head.

He was back in less than a minute, flickering candle-light now illuminating his tall figure and casting dark, dancing shadows on the wall. He went into the drawing-room, and she reluctantly trailed after him.

'Er—could you find a candle for me?' she asked rather edgily. 'Then I can find my way to my room.'

'Stay and have a drink first,' Maxim invited.

'No, thank you,' she said at once, 'I think I've already had enough.' They had had a bottle of wine with dinner, and she had drunk her fair share of it.

'Just a small brandy,' he said. 'It'll help you to relax.'

'I don't need to relax.'

'Oh, I think you do,' Maxim told her softly. Then he went over and closed the door, so that she couldn't leave the room.

'What are you doing?' she said, her nerves beginning to twitch anxiously.

'At the moment, nothing at all.' Maxim walked over, caught hold of her wrist, pulled her over to the sofa and sat her down. Then he seated himself beside her. 'But I do have plans for the rest of the evening,' he added.

'Plans?' she echoed edgily. 'What kind of plans?'

Maxim looked directly at her. 'I think you know exactly what plans I have in mind.'

And Cleo was very much afraid that she did. She tried to get to her feet—she supposed she had some idea about running away—but Maxim's fingers slid round her wrist again, holding her firmly in place.

'Perhaps you should have that brandy,' he suggested.

'Why do you want me to have another drink?'

'I told you, I want you to relax. You're completely well again now, so I think that it's time we crossed another hurdle. Only I ought to warn you that it's going to be a fairly major one, Cleo.'

Cleo's heart had begun to thud away quite painfully. 'I don't——' she began. Then she swallowed very hard, and got out, 'I don't want to cross *any* hurdles.'

'Yes, you do,' Maxim said with utter certainty. 'You're ready for it, you've been ready for longer than you think, but if you don't do it now—with me—then you might never find the nerve to do it. And that would be a terrible waste of your life.'

Something funny seemed to have happened to her breathing. And her legs were shaking, even though she was sitting down. All the same, she still wasn't ready to give up all her old fears and phobias.

'It's my life,' she said stubbornly. 'I can waste it, if I want to.'

'A couple of weeks ago, I'd probably have agreed with you. But it isn't just your life any more, it's mine as well.'

Cleo looked at him with wide eyes. 'What—what do you mean?'

The candle gave off barely enough light for her to see Maxim's face, but the dark glow in his eyes was clear enough, and so was the taut line of his mouth.

'You know very well what I mean,' he said after a short pause.

And she thought she did. But she still wanted to hear him say it.

'I don't know anything at all,' she lied. 'You'll have to tell me.'

His fingers tightened around her wrist. Then he began to speak in a level voice.

'It's been such a long time since I've wanted something—really wanted something—that I'd almost forgotten what it felt like. But I want you. After you'd only been here a couple of days, I knew that I wanted you. And not just in bed, although God knows I want that too.' His tone became more intense, with a raw edge to it. 'When my marriage went wrong, everything slowly seemed to fall apart, and I couldn't put it back together again. So I turned to my work—that became the most important thing in my life. That, and my children. Then Vivienne died, and for a long time I felt guilty as hell because I hadn't loved her for a long time, but nothing else changed, I seemed to have lost the ability to love and need and want. Perhaps the shock of losing my father at the same time helped to knock me even more emotionally off balance. I loved William and Alice, and I was fond of my sister and her family, but that was all, no one else could get near me. Oh, there were women in my life occasionally, but they were only brief affairs, unsatisfactory to everyone because I couldn't give and I couldn't take.'

Cleo listened to this admission with growing incredulity. He was telling her things that she knew he had never expected to admit to anyone.

Maxim paused for a moment; then he went on. 'When you first turned up on my doorstep, I told myself that you were shallow and self-centred, that you weren't even my type. I'd never been turned on by tall, slim blondes, no matter how beautiful they were. But there was something about you that got to me, a vulnerability in those damned green eyes of yours, something in the way you moved, spoke, even the way you argued with me. I told myself that I didn't need someone with so many hang-ups, that I still had enough problems of my own, I couldn't take on anyone else's. But then I kissed you, and that seemed to unlock something inside of me. For the first time in years I began to *feel*; it was as if the world had suddenly changed beneath my feet. I tried to fight it, but it was too late, it had already happened. After that I couldn't go back to the way I was before; I was lost—I'm still lost.'

'I—I wish that you hadn't told me all these things,' she said in a small, frightened voice.

'But I have. You told me once that I knew all your secrets. Now you know mine.'

His dark eyes burned into hers, and Cleo shivered. The pent-up passion inside him was finally breaking free—and she was the one who had done this to him. The thought both exhilarated and terrified her.

'I don't—don't know what to do,' she said haltingly.

'Don't do anything,' Maxim instructed softly. 'Let me do it all.'

He eased her back on to the couch, so that she was lying down. Then he stretched out beside her.

'Scared?' he said perceptively, as Cleo tried to still an inner trembling. 'Then I'll make you a promise. This will only go as far as you want it to go. Say stop at any time—and I will.' He looked at her intently. 'Do you believe that I'll keep my promise?'

She nodded, because she couldn't seem to get out any more words. Then she caught her breath because Maxim's hands had left her wrists, and were instead moving with intent over the soft material of her jogging suit.

He slid the sweatshirt over her head. 'Kick off those trainers,' he murmured. Numbly, Cleo obeyed. Then she found herself lifting her body so that he could ease the trousers over her hips. They were tossed to the floor, and she could feel the roughness of his jeans against her bare legs. And then the smoothness of his hand against the bare skin of her stomach.

She caught her breath. Lying in a man's arms, almost naked except for a couple of flimsy pieces of underwear—how could she do something so dangerous? But then she realised that the danger itself was arousing; she had lived a safe life for so long, and she was so *tired* of it—she suddenly craved more of this new kind of stimulation. But more important than that was the man who was providing it. Cleo knew that she couldn't have got even this far with anyone else. It had to be with someone she totally trusted—someone she loved. It had to be with Maxim...

His hands moved upwards, over the curve of her breast, and Cleo closed her eyes. Just the touch of his fingers was sweet, but then his mouth gently nibbled where his hands had been moments ago, provoking a deep ache of pleasure. Involuntarily her own hands moved towards him, began to slip inside the open neck of his shirt. He caught hold of them, though, and gently eased them away again.

'I told you,' he reminded her huskily, 'I don't want you to do anything. Except lie back, and relax. Enjoy.'

His mouth moved over her skin, his clever fingers coaxed pleasure from every inch of her body. Cleo floated on small waves of exquisite sensations. She hazily told herself that this ought to stop, it was going too far, but she couldn't resist the inexorable advance of his hands, and so Maxim was free to explore at leisure. And explore he did. From the soft swell of breast to the satin smoothness of inner thighs. From the sensitive soles of her feet to her gently trembling lips. And all the time he lay close, very close. Although he didn't remove a single item of his own clothes, Cleo was aware of the heated, hard arousal of his own body. And she also knew that his self-control was slowly slipping away from him.

Maxim raised himself on one elbow and looked down at her, his eyes glittering intensely.

'Still afraid, Cleo?' he challenged softly.

'Not—not of you,' she managed to get out. He had stopped caressing her and she was already missing the silken touch of his hands against her skin, her aroused body demanding more. But inside her head, there was still a small knot of the old fear that hadn't quite dissolved. It had been there for so very long, and no matter how overwhelming her new feelings were for this man, no matter that she knew very well that she was falling quite tumultuously in love with him, the fear that she had lived with all her adult life still held her back, and she just didn't have quite enough courage to take that last step.

Maxim began to touch her again, slowly stroking her stomach. 'I'd like to have another child with you,' he told her, his eyes never leaving her face. 'Perhaps it would have dark hair and green eyes. Or blonde hair and dark eyes. Can you picture a child like that, Cleo?'

'Yes,' she said in a shaken voice. And she could. Part of her even longed to touch it, hold it, something unique that she and Maxim had created between them. 'I never thought that I'd ever want something like that,' she went on unsteadily. 'I wouldn't *let* myself want it. But—oh, Maxim, I'm still scared, I can't *stop* being scared, even though I want to.' Unshed tears glistened brightly in her eyes. 'I don't know what to do,' she said despairingly.

Maxim's hand stilled for a moment; then he bent his head and lightly kissed her.

'It's all right,' he said. 'I know, I understand. You're not ready for that final risk, yet.'

'I'm just not brave enough,' Cleo whispered. 'And no matter how careful we are, no method of contraception is completely safe—there's always a small chance I could still get pregnant. And just the thought of it still terrifies me. I'm sorry,' she finished miserably.

Maxim gave her another kiss, longer, more intense than the last. 'There's no need to be sorry about anything,' he told her. 'Just relax and trust me. The rest of the night is still ahead of us, and I intend that we should enjoy every minute of it.'

Her eyes widened as she realised what he was telling her. That there were other ways in which they could share the pleasure of being together, other ways in which he would satisfy the newfound ache of love inside her.

Maxim's hand moved downwards from her stomach, dipped deeper into the heat that had begun to radiate from her body again, moved in a slow but purposeful caress that sent fresh waves of intense pleasure cascading from deep inside her. Cleo caught her breath, and her own hands began to move instinctively, restlessly, sliding beneath his clothing, fumbling with buttons and zips, finally finding the hard heat of his body against her fingertips.

His mouth drifted over her breasts, licked the hard tips into shivering pleasure, and then traced a path over the flat plane of her stomach. Cleo could hear her own fractured breathing and her fingers caressed him, tightened their grip.

A small, convulsive shudder ran though him and he caught hold of her wrist. 'Slowly,' he said shakily.

But there was too much pent-up love inside her, she couldn't seem to control it any more, she had been starved of this loving closeness all her life, and she was frantic to give love, take love.

Maxim seemed to know exactly what was happening to her because he released her wrist again. 'All right,' he said thickly, 'come to me now, Cleo, right now——'

He bent his head again, kissed the soft inner skin of her thighs, his tongue softly licked and tasted her, and an electrifying jolt of pleasure flashed through her, making her shake with its intensity. Then his mouth returned to her lips, she could taste the mingled scents of their bodies, and feel the heat that burned between them.

He stretched out beside her, moved closer, and she felt him fight back and control the urge simply to take her. Instead, he let her touch him as she pleased, lost in this new and fascinating exploration. He encouraged her when she hesitated, suddenly shy, licked and nibbled and provoked new tremors of response from her until she hovered on the very edge of a bottomless chasm. He kissed her over and over, kisses that became deeper and more intense, and his hands roamed over her with sweet intimacy until she could taste and touch and smell him, only him, nothing else seemed to exist for her. Then he briefly dragged his mouth away and his eyes burned down at her. 'Touch me again,' he ordered softly, his breath catching in his throat. 'Love me, Cleo.'

Cleo immediately obeyed, because she had already learned that pleasure had to be given, as well as taken, in order to be complete. But it was something that Maxim had known all along, and the sensual caresses of his fingers swiftly gathered together the small cascades of pleasure running through her and turned them into a sudden, overwhelming torrent as his own body shuddered helplessly again and again under her loving touch.

CHAPTER NINE

IN THE morning, Cleo felt too shy even to look at Maxim. And he seemed rather withdrawn, as if the intimacies of last night had left him unexpectedly off balance. There was a tension between them that hadn't been there during those long hours of darkness and shared secrets, and it seemed slowly to get worse, not better.

As they ate breakfast, neither of them speaking, she found herself staring at his hands. Such very clever hands. They could paint portraits that could reveal the sitter's soul. Put oil on canvas with such dexterity that painted skin could seem to breathe and eyes would glow with life. And they could make her, Cleo, cry out loud with love and pleasure.

Her throat tightened and she couldn't finish her coffee. She put the cup down rather unsteadily and wished that Maxim would say something—*anything*. But he remained silent, almost like a stranger. It was almost as if last night had never happened.

In the end, he did speak to her. But it was only to tell her that he was going to collect William and Alice, and he should be back in less than an hour.

After he had gone, the house seemed eerily silent. In the end, Cleo couldn't stand it and she went out into the garden.

Something was wrong, she told herself. No, *everything* was wrong, she conceded tiredly. It was time she admitted that to herself. This wasn't going to work, it couldn't work. Perhaps Maxim had already realised that.

That was why he was in such a strange mood this morning. And the fault was hers, of course.

He wanted more children, and she couldn't give them to him. He wanted to make love to her properly, but she was too scared to let him.

Cleo bowed her head. There were so many things wrong between them, and she couldn't put them right. If she loved him—and she knew now that she did—then she would want only what was best for him. And that wasn't an incomplete relationship that could go nowhere, and would only end up hurting both of them as Maxim became more and more frustrated, and she felt inadequate, a failure.

Better to end it now, before it deteriorated to that stage. Her old life was still waiting for her, back in London. She told herself that this was the time to go back to it. And her father was there, on his own, waiting for his daughter to come back home. He needed her, and Cleo had the feeling that she was rather desperately going to want to be needed in the next few weeks.

She began to walk back to the house. It would be easier for everyone if she went right now. Then she wouldn't have to face Maxim, go through all the tortuous explanations, perhaps have to listen to him trying to pretend that he didn't want her to go, trying to pretend that they could work this out.

Of course, it would mean that she wouldn't be able to say goodbye to William and Alice. That hurt, because she had started to love those children. And they would probably be sorry to find her gone when they returned home, but she told herself that they would soon get over it, they had their own friends, their own life, and they would both be back at school next week, which would give them plenty of other things to think about. They would miss her for a couple of days, but then they would forget her. But it would be a very long time before she forgot them.

Cleo went to her room and quickly packed. Should she leave a note? But what could she say? Anyway, Maxim would know why she had gone.

She hauled her case out to the car. Then she brushed her overbright eyes with the back of her hand. No time for tears, Maxim had already been gone for half an hour. She had to be well away from here before he returned.

She started up the engine of the small red sports car, but then just sat there for a couple of minutes. Actually to drive away from the house was even harder than she had expected. It had to be done, though. She revved up the engine fiercely, and then let the car abruptly hurtle down the drive.

The journey back to London was one that she could never remember at all clearly afterwards. It was probably a miracle that she reached home without being involved in a major accident.

Cleo tiredly got out and walked up to the front door. She fumbled for her key, then let herself in. And it was funny, but the house that had been her home all her life, with its exquisite furnishings and priceless ornaments and paintings, seemed almost unfamiliar.

She hoped her father wasn't at home. She needed a couple of hours on her own, to wash away the fatigue of the journey and try to do something about the even deeper fatigue in her soul. As she walked down the hall, though, the door of the drawing-room opened and her father came out.

'Cleo!' he said in surprise. 'What on earth are you doing here?'

It wasn't the kind of reception she had been expecting. Her father sounded almost as if he was not very pleased to see her. And Cleo suddenly realised that he hadn't phoned her once, during the time she had been at Maxim's house. The only time that she had spoken to him was when she had rung him. That wasn't like him. He usually liked to keep in touch every couple of days.

'I came back early——' she began to say, but then stopped, because her father wasn't on his own.

A woman had followed him out of the drawing-room. She was in her late thirties, well-dressed, pleasant-looking, and had bright, intelligent eyes and a friendly smile.

'Hello,' she said. 'We haven't met before, although your father has told me a great deal about you.'

Her father looked oddly ill at ease. 'Cleo, this is Laura Brenton. She's a—very good friend of mine. Laura, you already know that this is Cleo, my daughter.'

'I'm pleased to meet you at last,' said Laura. Then she turned back to Cleo's father. 'Look, I'm sorry, but I really do have to go. I've a very important appointment; I can't miss it. I'll see you tomorrow?'

'Yes, of course,' her father said at once.

'Goodbye, Cleo,' Laura said, her voice low and charming. 'I'm sorry to dash off as soon as we've met, but I expect we'll have a chance to talk together fairly soon.'

As Laura left, Cleo gave a puzzled frown. What was going on here?

When her father returned from seeing Laura out, Cleo followed him into the drawing-room.

'I didn't expect you back yet,' said her father, pouring himself a drink. 'Is the portrait finished?'

'The portrait?' she echoed. She had almost forgotten about it. 'No,' she went on rather shakily, remembering *why* the portrait was still unfinished. 'And I don't think that it will be now——' She broke off, not knowing where to start. 'Look, I'm sorry about the portrait,' she said at last.

Her father shrugged. 'It isn't important.'

At that, Cleo's head shot up. 'What do you mean, it isn't important? You really pressured me to go up there, to have it painted. And you bribed Maxim——' oh, God, it was difficult to say his name! '—you bribed him to paint it by giving a huge donation to the Brenner Trust,' she finally managed to finish.

Her father looked apologetic. 'I'll be honest with you, Cleo. Yes, I did want that portrait. But I also wanted to get you out of the house for a week or two. And when you caught that flu virus and had to stay at Maxim Brenner's even longer—well, I'm sorry you were ill, of course, but in a way it was rather fortunate. You see, Laura and I—well, we've only recently met, it was while you were on that modelling assignment in Bermuda, but things moved very quickly—and it's difficult—I mean, with your daughter under the same roof——'

Cleo sat down very abruptly. 'I don't believe this,' she said rather shrilly. 'You wanted me out of the house so you could have an affair with Laura Brenton?'

Her father immediately shot a stern look at her. 'This isn't just an affair, Cleo. We're in love. So, please be careful how you talk about Laura in the future.'

But Cleo was too shocked to say anything more at all, at the moment.

'I never expected anything like this to happen,' her father went on, beginning to sound a little awkward again. 'But it has, and I'm afraid you'll just have to accept it. I know it'll be hard for you, because we've always been very close. Perhaps too close—maybe I should have tried to make you stand on your own two feet before this. But you were a rather lonely child, Cleo, and you always seemed so dependent on me. But you're an adult now, and I think that it really is time that you—that we both—began to live our own lives.'

She suppressed the urge to laugh rather hysterically. All those years when she had convinced herself that she couldn't leave her father because he was dependent on her. But he hadn't been dependent at all, he had been patiently waiting for her to grow up and claim her own independence!

'I think you'll like Laura, once you get to know her,' he went on with more confidence. 'I know that she isn't beautiful, but she's warm, she's loving, and to be perfectly honest, I adore her.'

'But—my mother——' Cleo said, in a rather tight voice.

'You know that I loved your mother,' her father said at once. 'But she's been dead for eighteen years, Cleo. And they've been very lonely years for me.'

'You had me,' she said, deeply hurt by that last remark.

'Yes, I know,' he said, 'and I've loved you, and thanked God that your mother was brave enough to give you to me. But I still feel the need to share my life with another adult. Surely you're old enough now to understand that?'

But Cleo only half heard that last question. Her sharp mind had latched on to what he had said just before that.

'What do you mean—about my mother being brave enough to give me to you?' she said, looking straight at her father.

'That she knew the risk involved, of course. I never wanted her to have children at all, I wanted her to follow the doctors' advice, but she was so determined—and what your mother wanted, she usually got,' he said with a wry smile. 'She was so strong-willed; it was one of the things I loved and admired about her.'

Cleo began to feel shocked all over again. She had always thought that her mother had been a rather gentle, submissive woman, who had given in to the forceful demands of her father. Of course, no one had actually ever told her that—her father had spoken so little about her—but the dreamy-eyed portrait that hung in the drawing-room certainly gave that impression. And what was this about a risk?

'You said that you wanted her to follow the doctors' advice,' she said slowly, at last. '*What* advice?'

Her father sighed. 'Your mother suffered from hypertension—that's abnormally high blood-pressure. It's unusual in someone as young as she was, but it does happen. And, since pregnancy can cause sudden, steep rises in blood-pressure, the dangers were obvious. With you, we were lucky—there weren't any problems that the doctors couldn't cope with. I didn't want to tempt fate again, we already had one beautiful, healthy child, but your mother was absolutely determined to have a second baby.'

Cleo was stunned. Her mother hadn't died simply as a result of childbirth? Her state of health had already been precarious? But it seemed that she had been so determined to give her husband another child that she had simply ignored the risks, and gone ahead with the pregnancy.

'Why—why didn't you tell me all this before?' she said, in a shaken voice.

'I felt guilty that I had given in, allowed her to have the baby,' her father admitted. 'Guilty that I'd made her pregnant in the first place. It seemed to make me responsible for her death. In the end, the only way I could cope with what happened to your mother was to push it to the very back of my mind, try not to talk about it or even think about it.'

'I wish you'd told me all this years ago,' Cleo sighed.

'I wanted to, I kept telling myself that I *would* tell you as soon as you were old enough to understand, but the longer I left it, the harder it got. I'm sorry, Cleo,' he said simply.

'I think that I need time to think all this over,' she said, with a tired shake of her head. 'Can I stay here for a while? Will you and Laura mind?'

'This is your home,' her father said at once. 'You can stay here for as long as you like.'

But Cleo knew that she would eventually have to move out. She was finally beginning to break the ties with her childhood, with the past. Only, at the moment, she didn't seem to have a future.

For the next few days, she moved around as if in a dream. She met Laura again, and found herself almost unwillingly liking her. She rang up friends, but then couldn't seem to talk to them. Didn't even bother to phone back when the model agency got in touch, to ask if she was available for more work. Her life seemed to have dropped into limbo, and she couldn't summon up enough energy, enough enthusiasm to do anything about it.

She knew that she ought to start looking for a place of her own, a flat or perhaps a small house. She registered with a couple of estate agents, but then couldn't be bothered to look at the properties they recommended. And all the time, she refused to think about the one thing that did really matter: the way she had walked out on Maxim, without even saying goodbye. But what else could she have done? She was making such a mess of her own life; how could she ruin his as well?

The rest of the week drifted past, the empty days running into one another, the nights long and miserable. And her father was so wrapped up in his relationship with Laura that he didn't even seem to notice that she was looking pale and listless. That hurt for a while, because she was so used to having his undivided attention. Then she straightened her shoulders and told herself that she had better get used to it. From now on, she was going to have to share him.

At the end of the week, Cleo got up late—it was getting to be an effort just to get out of bed in the morning—pulled on a dressing-gown, and was just despondently making her way downstairs when there was a short, hard knock at the front door.

As her father went to open it, she hesitated halfway down the stairs, not wanting any visitors to see her like this, undressed and with her hair still tangled after yet another restless night.

Then her entire nervous system went into shock as she heard a familiar voice.

'I've come for Cleo,' Maxim stated unequivocally.

'And you are?' asked her father politely.

'Maxim Brenner. I've brought the portrait you commissioned. But, in return, I want the real thing.'

'You'd better come in,' her father said in a rather bemused voice. 'I'm afraid that Cleo isn't up yet.'

'Yes—yes, I am,' she said in a quavery voice, holding on to the banisters because her legs suddenly felt horribly weak and trembly. She went down the last few stairs, and she could see Maxim now. He was standing in the entrance hall, as tall, as dark, as overwhelmingly familiar as she remembered him. His eyes swung round to fix on her, and she shook all over again under the intensity of his gaze.

'Go and get dressed,' Maxim instructed her calmly. 'We have to leave almost immediately. I have to get back before William and Alice return home from school.'

'I—I can't go anywhere with you,' she stuttered.

'I think you should certainly get dressed,' her father told her. 'We can discuss the other matter afterwards.' Then he turned back to Maxim. 'Perhaps you'd like to come and wait in the drawing-room? You can show me the portrait, and I'll get my housekeeper to make some coffee.'

Cleo staggered back upstairs on legs that still refused to function properly. In a total daze, she showered, brushed her hair, pulled on jeans and a sweater, then stared at her reflection in the mirror.

Wide, disbelieving eyes stared back at her. Maxim here? At her house? Demanding that she return home with him?

Still not quite believing that any of this was happening, she went downstairs to join her father and Maxim.

They were drinking coffee, and the portrait that Maxim had painted of her was propped up on the table. Cleo gazed at it for a long time. She looked very young, very vulnerable, very beautiful in an untouched way, not at all like the sophisticated model who smiled out from the pages of glossy magazines.

'Not quite what I expected,' said her father drily, also looking at the portrait. 'But I like it. I like it a lot. Mr Brenner's captured something that I've never seen in you before. I wish that he could have painted a portrait of your mother. That painting of her is a very good physical likeness, but it doesn't capture her spirit and her character.' He put down his coffee and looked directly at Cleo. 'Mr Brenner is quite insistent that he's taking you back with him. How do you feel about that?'

'Well—I'm n-not going, of course,' she stuttered.

'I think you should consider it,' her father said calmly, to her amazement. Then he glanced at his watch. 'Look, I'm afraid I have to go out, I'm meeting Laura in quarter of an hour. I'll leave the two of you to talk this over. If you decide to leave with Mr Brenner, Cleo, give me a ring later on and let me know where you are.'

She gaped at him. 'You'd just let me walk out of here with him? Someone you don't even know?'

'I know *you*, Cleo. And I've seen how miserable you've been these last few days. I think Mr Brenner can do something about that. And as for letting you walk out of here with him—remember, I'm an excellent judge of character,' her father said. 'I'm sure that you'll be perfectly safe in his hands. And he *does* seem extremely determined to have you,' he added, with a grin. Then he left them alone together.

Cleo found that she couldn't look directly at Maxim. 'Thank you for bringing the portrait,' she mumbled at last.

'I could have brought it sooner,' he told her. 'I finished it a couple of days ago. But I thought you might need some more time on your own, to get a few things straight.'

'What sort of things?' she asked warily.

'For a start, what you intend to do with the rest of your life.'

She bit her lip. 'I haven't decided that yet.'

'No, I rather thought not,' Maxim said levelly. 'That's why I'm making the decision for you.'

'You've no right to do that!' she said indignantly.

In two strides, he was standing in front of her, his dark eyes no longer so calm. 'Since we're talking about rights, don't you think that *I* have the right to know why you walked out without any warning? Not even a note or a phone call, to say why you'd gone?'

'You *know* why I left!'

'I certainly don't. And don't try and tell me it was because of that night we spent together. You weren't frightened of what we did that night, in fact I could probably have taken it a lot further, only I didn't want to push you too far, too fast.'

Cleo went scarlet as she remembered that night. 'But it couldn't have been good for you,' she mumbled at last, still refusing to look at his face. 'It wasn't what you really wanted, you couldn't have gone on being satisfied with just that.'

'Why not let me be the judge of what satisfies me?' Maxim demanded.

'And there's the question of children,' she went on stubbornly. 'You want more, you know you do. And I don't know if I can——' Her voice trailed away because, somehow, the idea wasn't quite as frightening as it had once been. That was so extraordinary that she had to stop and consider it for a few moments.

Maxim was already speaking again, though. And this time he hooked his finger under her chin, forcing her head up so that she had to look directly into his blazing eyes.

'Let me *tell* you what I want,' he said fiercely. 'For a start, I want you. I told you that, but perhaps I didn't make myself clear. I want the whole package, hang-ups, fears and phobias, as well as the good parts. Half-satisfactory lovemaking with you is still better than being completely intimate with anyone else. You satisfy me in ways that have nothing to do with being in bed together. And as for this question of children, I don't want you because I want to breed a whole line of Brenners. I've got William and Alice, and they can be more than enough for me, if they have to be.' He shook her a little roughly. 'Do you understand what I'm saying to you, Cleo?'

She was beginning to realise that she did. But she still wasn't sure that she quite believed it.

'But that morning I left—you were in such an odd mood,' she said hesitantly. 'You seemed to have withdrawn from me completely, I thought—well, that you'd realised what a poor deal you'd be getting, if you took me on.'

Maxim ran his fingers through his black hair. 'You couldn't have been more wrong. I was silent because I didn't know what to say to you. That night we spent together—it was totally different from any other night I've ever spent, but I didn't know how to tell you. I'd run right out of words. And *you* were so quiet that I began to wonder if I'd pushed you too far, too fast, and that scared the hell out of me, I didn't want to frighten you away and lose you. In the end, I decided to fetch William and Alice. I thought that, once they were around, we'd start to talk normally to each other again, and I'd finally be able to tell you all the things I wanted to say. But when I got back to the house with them, you'd gone. I was devastated, and so were the kids. Alice has been crying ever since you left, and even William's been walking round with a quivering bottom lip.'

Cleo gulped. 'I didn't mean to upset everyone so much.'

'Then come back with me, and put things right,' he said huskily. 'We all need you, Cleo.'

She was silent for a few seconds. Then, in a small voice, she said, 'All right. I'll come.'

After that, everything seemed to get very confused for a very long while. She remembered Maxim kissing her—yes, she certainly remembered that!—and she recalled throwing a lot of clothes haphazardly into a couple of cases, then she was in Maxim's car and it was powerfully eating up the miles on the motorway as they headed back north.

And the sun was still shining, not a drop of rain in sight, when they finally reached the Lake District. The water of the lakes glittered tranquilly, the mountains rose up into the blue sky and shimmered in the haze, the fields were a brilliant green and the trees still clung to their summer foliage, resisting the pull of autumn.

Maxim finally pulled up outside the house and then carried in her cases. Cleo followed more slowly, trying to convince herself that she actually was here.

'When will William and Alice be home?' she asked a little hesitantly, feeling strangely shy at being alone here with Maxim.

He turned and his dark eyes briefly glittered. 'Not until tomorrow. While you were packing, I phoned Sarah and asked if she would collect them from school, and keep them overnight. I thought that we needed some time on our own,' he went on. 'Once William and Alice are here, we won't get another chance to be together all night until we've made this completely legal.'

Cleo swallowed hard. 'Legal as in—married?' she said shakily.

'Of course,' Maxim answered at once. 'I'm trying to teach my kids some of the old-fashioned values. And it's going to be hard to do that if they find out their father's living in sin,' he finished with a sudden grin.

'But I haven't said—I mean, you haven't even asked——'

'We don't need to go through the formalities,' he interrupted calmly. 'This is right for both of us, Cleo.' He picked up her cases again. 'I'll put these in the annexe,' he added. 'I'm afraid you'll have to stay there until I manage to fix up the ceremony and officially turn you into Mrs Brenner.'

Cleo Brenner—it already sounded right. She wandered after Maxim, into the annexe, with some vague notion about unpacking. Before she could open one of the cases, though, Maxim moved closer, and she could feel that his body was already hot, see that his eyes were very bright.

'I've missed you,' he murmured. 'Missed being near to you.'

Cleo found that her skin felt raw, as if it were waiting to be soothed by his touch. And she didn't have to wait long. His hands slid over her with sudden intensity and he seemed suddenly overwhelmed by an urgent need for her; he kissed her over and over, long, dark kisses that left them both shaking a little. Then he abruptly let go of her.

'No—don't——' she found herself whispering.

'I've got to,' he said jerkily. 'Or I might not be able to keep my promise.'

'What promise?' she said in confusion.

'Always to stop when you want me to.'

'But I don't want you to stop,' Cleo said shakily.

'Think what you're saying,' he warned her.

She buried her head against her shoulder, hopelessly shy. 'I know what I'm saying,' she told him in a voice muffled by his body.

She felt Maxim catch his breath sharply. 'Nothing's changed, Cleo. All the old risks, however small, that you were so frightened of are still there. I can't make them go away. I can be careful, but I can't give you any absolute guarantees against pregnancy.'

'I don't want you to.' She raised her head slowly. 'I found something out about my mother in these last few days,' she told him. 'She was very brave, much braver than I'll probably ever be. I suppose that I always thought of her as a victim, giving my father another child because it was what *he* wanted, and never dreaming that it was going to kill her. Perhaps that even helped to make me frightened of men, the thought that they could make you love them so much that they could persuade you to do anything for them. But I was totally wrong, it wasn't like that at all. She was the one who wanted the child, she knew that it was dangerous because of her health, but she still went ahead; she was willing to take a chance. She wanted to live her life to the full, no matter what the consequences. And I think that it's about time I did the same. Yes, I'm still scared,' she admitted frankly, 'but when I'm with you, I get a little less scared all the time. You give me the courage to do things that I thought I was never going to do.'

'Then let's take this one step at a time,' he said quietly. 'Trust me to take all the necessary precautions, and if at some time in the future you feel ready to go any further, to take that next big step, just tell me to stop.' Cleo silently nodded, and he bent his head and swiftly kissed her. Then he said, 'Wait here for a moment.'

He was back in less than a minute. Then he slowly gathered her to him, his arms came up and locked her against him. And the kiss that he then gave her was different from any he had ever given her before.

Cleo found herself lowered to the bed, her clothes removed with growing impatience, but it didn't matter, she was already helping with buttons and catches. And Maxim's own clothes were soon discarded, and she was free to explore the hard lines of his body, feel the smooth heat of his skin under her palms, and it *was* frightening, but only because it was all still so new to her. And the reason for his brief exit became clear as he paused for just a few seconds to quickly and easily take care of the precautions he had promised. Then he turned back to her, his eyes bright, his breathing as unsteady as her own, and his hands already reaching for her.

And then everything suddenly became turbulent and chaotic, too many desires pent up for too long and they all seemed to break free at once. Afterwards, she could only remember vivid moments; Maxim's mouth against her breasts, her thighs, his fingers caressing her into arousal so that she was ready for him, her own fingers touching his hard body and the convulsive shudder that ran through him. Heat and sweat, hot skin, and fingers tangled in damp hair. Kisses that left lips bruised, but aching for more. The unfamiliar pressure of a male body, an unexpected moment of pain, and a few moments of stillness until he was sure she was all right. Then quickening movements, deep inner shivers and dark, intense pleasures that escalated until they were out of control. Everything falling apart, dizzying sensations, and then that new pleasure that she had experienced with him once before, even more intense this time, and so intimate that everything else faded into insignificance, and the world changed forever for Cleo.

Falling asleep in Maxim's arms, exhausted, safe, loved. And waking up again some time later to find that he was still there, it hadn't all been some wild and impossible figment of her imagination.

'After this, I might ask my sister to keep William and Alice for a whole week,' Maxim murmured.

'No, I want to see them,' Cleo told him. 'But not until tomorrow,' she added, rather dreamily. 'Tonight belongs to us.'

'And you belong to me,' he told her, tightening his grip on her.

'Yes, I know,' she said simply. 'I don't know why it took me so long to realise that.'

'I was afraid that you might never realise it,' he said rather huskily. 'Or be too afraid to admit it.'

'Right now, I don't feel afraid of anything. And I don't feel like the same person I was a few weeks ago.'

'Don't change too much,' he told her. 'I like the Cleo I've got right now. And I'd like to paint you the way you look at this moment,' he added. 'Your skin flushed, your lips and breasts swollen, the marks of my hands on your body. You look so beautiful, every inch of you glows. And you're blushing,' he said with some satisfaction. 'I've always wanted to marry a girl who can blush.'

'If you keep saying those kind of things to me, I'll be doing it all the time,' she warned. Then she looked up at him. 'Will you keep saying them?'

'I think that I can guarantee that your face will be permanently red in the future,' Maxim said with a grin. Then his expression changed. 'And for the first time in years, I'm looking forward to that future,' he said more softly. 'That's what you've done for me, Cleo.' He bent his head and kissed her, and the kiss slowly deepened into the irresistible desire that went with love.

Cleo surrendered to it with sweet abandon. No more fears, no holding back. This was where her life began, with this man, with his children—and perhaps, even her own children. And she thought fleetingly of her mother, who had lived her own brave life to the full. Then she turned to Maxim, and thought only of the future.

EPILOGUE

CLEO sat on a rug in the garden in the warm sunshine, savouring the few minutes of peace. This was her third autumn in the Lake District, and it was her favourite season, with its gentle sunshine and warm colours.

Beside her, wrapped in a light blanket and fast asleep, lay Kate Brenner. Three months old and, in Cleo's biased opinion, the most beautiful baby in the world. Cleo gently touched Kate's dark hair, and waited impatiently for her to wake up so that she could see her eyes, which were one day going to be as green as her mother's.

Having her hadn't been easy, of course. Cleo had been terrified as many times as she had been excited, once the pregnancy—the planned pregnancy—had been confirmed. But Maxim had been there every step of the way, right up until the moment when Kate had been born, yelling her head off in protest at having to leave the warm security of her mother's body.

Maxim had arranged for her to have the baby at home, so that she wouldn't have to cope with the added pressure of going into hospital. That had also meant that William and Alice could see their new sister almost immediately she was born, which had thrilled them, and made them feel closer to the latest addition to their family. Everything had worked out so well that Cleo was already thinking that she might just want to do it all over again, in a couple of years' time. A boy would be nice, next time...

'You're smiling,' Maxim murmured, sitting down beside her. 'Thinking about me?'

'In a way,' Cleo said with an answering grin. Then she gave a small sigh of satisfaction. 'This is a lovely day.'

'We could make it even nicer,' he said, twisting a strand of her pale blonde hair around his finger.

'How?'

'William and Alice won't be home from school for another couple of hours. And Kate's just been fed. If we put her in her cot, she'll sleep soundly for the rest of the afternoon,' he said persuasively.

'And what would we do with all this free time?'

'I could work on the portrait I'm painting of you and the children. Or we could do something much more interesting,' he suggested, letting his finger trail over the warm nape of her neck.

Cleo's body responded as it always did to his touch, with a small shiver of pleasure.

'I do love you,' she said softly.

'I know,' said Maxim with some satisfaction, as he got to his feet. He picked up his daughter, caught hold of his wife's hand, and took them both inside the house.

Next Month's Romances

Each month you can choose from a wide variety of romance with Mills & Boon. Below are the new titles to look out for next month, why not ask either Mills & Boon Reader Service or your Newsagent to reserve you a copy of the titles you want to buy – just tick the titles you would like and either post to Reader Service or take it to any Newsagent and ask them to order your books.

Please save me the following titles:	Please tick	√
HIGH RISK	Emma Darcy	
PAGAN SURRENDER	Robyn Donald	
YESTERDAY'S ECHOES	Penny Jordan	
PASSIONATE CAPTIVITY	Patricia Wilson	
LOVE OF MY HEART	Emma Richmond	
RELATIVE VALUES	Jessica Steele	
TRAIL OF LOVE	Amanda Browning	
THE SPANISH CONNECTION	Kay Thorpe	
SOMETHING MISSING	Kate Walker	
SOUTHERN PASSIONS	Sara Wood	
FORGIVE AND FORGET	Elizabeth Barnes	
YESTERDAY'S DREAMS	Margaret Mayo	
STORM OF PASSION	Jenny Cartwright	
MIDNIGHT STRANGER	Jessica Marchant	
WILDER'S WILDERNESS	Miriam Macgregor	
ONLY TWO CAN SHARE	Annabel Murray	

If you would like to order these books in addition to your regular subscription from Mills & Boon Reader Service please send £1.80 per title to: Mills & Boon Reader Service, Freepost, P.O. Box 236, Croydon, Surrey, CR9 9EL, quote your Subscriber No:................................. (If applicable) and complete the name and address details below. Alternatively, these books are available from many local Newsagents including W.H.Smith, J.Menzies, Martins and other paperback stockists from 14th May 1993.

Name:...

Address:...

....Post Code:.........................

To Retailer: If you would like to stock M&B books please contact your regular book/magazine wholesaler for details.

You may be mailed with offers from other reputable companies as a result of this application. If you would rather not take advantage of these opportunities please tick box ☐